Driftwood

Tony Cameron was born in Melbourne, Australia. He escaped in his early twenties to central Victoria years before the big 'tree change'. He designed and built a sustainable house, and raised two sustainable children.

Tony worked for twenty years in the performing arts world as a sound engineer, lighting tech, tour manager and head tech. He recently relocated to Thailand where he spends his time scouring the beaches for treasures.

www.amazon.com/author/anthonyscameron

Driftwood

by

Anthony S Cameron

For my daughters, Cass and Hannah, without whom the child within me would have disappeared years ago.
I would also like to thank my fiancé Roxy Hichens for her love, support and incredible editing skills.

A Beach in Thailand
Present

The waves hit the beach with the pent-up fury of a thousand defeated men. I am staring out at them, lost in thought. I feel disconnected and yet I can feel the sand under my feet as I walk. I can hear my friends walking next to me. I can smell the salt and rotten debris, which is scattered along the entire beach. I feel like I am dreaming this moment and these friends around me are a figment of my imagination. The ocean is a swollen pregnant thing; huge waves approach the sand with an ominous grin, then merely hiss as they hit land, a long powerful hiss that sweeps up the beach as we walk, then gets drowned out by the roar of a jet engine as a plane lurches up into the air, over the ocean to some other place.

The sun rises up over a bulging equatorial horizon and splashes the beach with an orange light that illuminates the tops of the waves as they make their sullen journey to the beach. Each wave deposits more debris, more treasures for my friends and me to collect. Already, our arms are laden with various things, mostly broken pieces of fishing boats and trees, which we guess are coming from Burma. My friends walk ahead of me now and I can hear their shrieks of delight as another piece reveals itself to them. I walk quite slowly along the beach but my thoughts race. I can hear a song vividly in my head, Dirty Three's "Everything's Fucked", a combination of grungy semi-acoustic guitar, sparse drums played with brushes that seem to follow the pulse, and a wailing, distorted violin. A smile spreads across my face, I look out at the pregnant ocean and it is then that I see it. I stand staring at it now, watching it

7

being caressed by the ocean, rolling over and over, out of time with the waves. I let go of the pile of driftwood in my hands and listen for the sound of them hitting the sand, but I hear nothing apart from the hiss of the waves and the song in my head. Even the sounds of my friends exploring the debris seem muffled and strangely distant, like when you hear the reverb on a vocal, all on its own. Now I sit gazing at this giant log in the water. My smile is now a grin. Tears are rolling down my cheeks...

The Release
5 years ago

The house lights go down slowly and the audience stop talking as they are plunged into darkness. I look at the mixing console, place two fingers lightly on the mute buttons, turn around to Johnno, the lighting guy, and say: "Let's do this thing!"

I hit the buttons and soon after the low rumble of a Hammond organ can be heard. I slowly bring the faders up and the rumble fills the room, shaking the walls. I can feel it through my fingers as I open up the orchestra channels. It is almost too much and I grin as I see some audience members squirming uncomfortably in their seats. I fade the rumble two beats before the band kicks in, crafting an eerie momentary silence... and then they're in the mix, well rehearsed and perfectly balanced. They are well into the intro to "Jesus Christ Superstar" when the curtains are pulled back and the theatre is bathed in a blue light as "JC" strides onto stage and launches into the first song. The orchestra is cooking; the vocal strong, gutsy; the reverb I have added dripping off his voice in time with the music. I am buzzing.

"Got 'em," I say to Johnno over the cans and he nods, playing with his nose ring whilst riding faders.

"*Got 'em.*" I say to myself.

***

It is 2a.m. I am driving home, sipping a bourbon and smoking a joint as my car careers through the central Victorian night. Kangaroos grazing by the roadside look up startled as I shoot past, and as each one passes I say, "Thank you, my friend" for the pleasure of not having one of them jump out in front of me. My ears are ringing from the gig and all I can hear is the low whoosh of rubber on a cold road. I get an image of Lisa looking out of the window through the grey drizzle whilst cuddling Lenny, her cross-eyed dog. My phone rings and I struggle to find the drinks holder and keep a hand on the wheel as I reach into my pocket and retrieve it. It is her.

"Wow, I was just thinking about you!" probably shouting due to the ear pounding of the gig.

"Baby, when you coming home... I wanna see you..."

"Soon baby, soon. On my way now... you waitin' up for me?"

She sighs, and I can't work out if it is a sexy sigh or a frustrated sigh.

"Yeah baby, I need to see you."

I hang up and reach for my drink and I picture her naked body walking towards me, wet from the shower and smiling. I put the foot down.

I open the front door quietly. I can hear Lenny growling from the bedroom. I put my gear on the kitchen table and finally let out an exhausted sigh as I look around at this house I built. I look at the smooth hand-rendered walls, the recycled windows. I look at the warm, welcoming lounge with the fire dying slowly, leaving a dull red glow through the glass door of the fireplace. As I remove my boots, I hear the squeak of the bedroom door and then she is walking towards me wearing knickers and a singlet. I can see her nipples poking through the material and she has a sexy smile on her face. Lenny is licking my feet and wagging his tail…

Now we are in the bedroom and her legs are pressing up against the wall as I slowly kiss her body. I can feel them trembling slightly. I let my lips just touch the skin on her belly and goose bumps rise up to greet me and as I enter her slowly she grabs me and pulls me in hard, grabbing my cock with so much force I feel like it is going to burst. I can feel her pleasure building and building until I know there is no going back for her and as she starts to come I come with her and her body becomes electrified, she trembles and shakes and cries and bites my shoulder hard. It lasts for a long time and I start to worry she is having a seizure. Her body has a film of sweat covering it and she looks at me, startled, wondering herself: how long can an orgasm last? Finally we are spent, her legs now hang limply off the bed – her pussy raised, swollen and still throbbing. We lie silently in the darkness for some time. And then she says,

"I'm leaving you."

<u>Sledgehammer</u>
40 years ago

I reach up onto my tiptoes to flush the toilet. As I do, I hear the smash of glass falling to the ground. I open the door and I see the glass shards on the floor opposite me a few feet away, and a large hairy hand reaching through the broken pane... The hand is reaching for the door lock as my heart pounds and my 4-year-old legs carry me screaming through the kitchen and into the lounge room where my Mum and her best friend, Nadia, are sitting. My look of fear and panic infect the room; they both jump to their feet as the sledgehammer my father is carrying hits its first target, the hot water service... I can hear the steam hissing out of it from where I stand, frozen, numbed, trapped inside the reverberation of the first blow...

He is silent except for the grunts as he smashes everything around him. My Mum is running into the bedroom where my brother and sister are sleeping. Nadia is frantically trying to get her fingers to stop shaking so she can dial the emergency number. It's one of those phones that you put your finger in the digit you want and wind it around to the little tab and then wait until it springs back before you can dial another. And the number she is dialling is 000, the furthest number away from the little tab.

My father has made it to the kitchen now and I can hear doors being ripped off their hinges, plates being broken, benches being smashed to pieces and the slow click... click... click... of the phone springing back.

Liquid Moments
16 years ago

My car lurches up the driveway under the weight of rocks. I gun the motor and come to an abrupt halt just past one of the last clear strips of ground left. I clamber out of the car and the dogs climb out through the open windows. Looking down the driveway I survey the many piles of rocks I have been depositing here, all the various shapes and textures and colours all piled up on top of one another. I hear the fly-wire door bouncing shut and see my girls running towards me.

"Daaaaaaaaddy!"

Hannah is the first to make it and envelopes me in one of her famous bear hugs, leaping fully off the ground at the last moment. Cass isn't far behind and I see the excited look on her face as she hugs the bottom half of me. The dogs trot playfully around our feet, Pepe jumping up onto the trailer upon which I am leaning and trying to join in.

"Hey girls, guess what? " I hear myself saying.

"What Daddy?" they shout in unison.

"I'm thinking about going on an adventure, wanna come?" I can feel my eyes widen as I say 'adventure'.

"Oh yes, yes!" they reply.

"Awesome, then why don't you change into your adventure clothes, I'll unload the trailer and I'll meet you right here, OK?"

As they run off, the dogs follow, nipping at their ankles as they go. I turn around smiling to myself and start tossing the sandstone rocks off the trailer onto the ground.

***

"Dad?" Cass says, "I was wondering about something."

"Yessss?" I say playfully as I navigate the turn off that will lead us into the bush.

"Yesterday I was lying on the trampoline and I was watching the clouds going past me and I thought 'Why am I here? What am I here for?' And like, how many rocks do we need to build our house with Daddy?"

I look over at her from the drivers seat and smile lovingly at my 7-year-old daughter and watch her blond wisps of hair being blown about by the wind as the scrappy, dry regrowth turns into a pine plantation.

"Lots of rocks, darling. Lots and lots…"

"What sort of rocks are we looking for, Daddy?" Han asks from the back seat.

"Just beautiful ones, sweetheart."

"How do we know which ones are beautiful, Daddy?"

"Don't worry, you will know when you see them…"

The Raffle
20 years ago

The ambulance bounces over a rough patch of highway and it is like a sledgehammer blow to my arm. It even shakes the doctor off her seat and into the side wall. As I scream and writhe in the stretcher I catch a glimpse of a stockinged leg rearranging itself... The sledgehammer starts up again; everything is getting darker, her voice is saying, as if she were miles away:

"Get the Narcan he's fading on us..."

That's all I know for a while...

***

When I wake up it is two days later. I am still screaming. I look at my arm. Thank Christ, still there. The sledgehammer has become a red -hot poker being scraped along my arm. My arm is all wrapped up and blood had soaked through the bandages. I am in a bed in a Melbourne hospital. A nurse comes in and plunges a needle into my leg.

"Morphine" she says.

"Thank you" I reply.

I look around the room. A great surge of relief is burning its way up from my leg. It feels good. The sun is struggling through the brown haze outside. The man next to me coughs and splutters; building up to a huge choking noise and then I hear something splatter onto a bedpan.

There is another man, or what is left of one, across from me. He is all curled up in a ball and staring vacantly down the corridor. Next to his bed is an artificial leg resting, in an almost dignified way, against a chair...

A Beach in Thailand
Present

Tears are pouring down my cheeks, and yet I am not sad. I am smiling, or rather, grinning. I remember having this feeling before, after seeing Cass draw her first breath as the street sweepers' lights beat on the window pane of the city hospital. Afterwards I remember sitting in a doorway on the street outside the hospital at 5a.m and writing... the tears had gone, the grin hadn't, and it was poetry that landed on the page. It was the feeling of being caught up in a larger moment.

And this time, it's this log, this lolling chunk of rainforest that sets me off. The sun has hit the water and the log glistens as it is picked up by the waves, the way a ballet dancer picks up a ballerina in a smooth, powerful and languid way. It is a dance, a beautiful dance I am watching. The log seems to resist, like a shy lover who feigns disinterest...

A Desert and a Slide Guitar
4 years ago

The four of us are standing on the loading dock out the back of the theatre watching the truck reverse into position. With a clunk, the tailgate hits the rubber blocks and at last the relentless beeping of the truck ceases. Two young techs jump out of the truck, the usual kind… scraggy black hair, piercings, and the wild look of being on tour for six months. We all introduce ourselves and then Geoff, the tour manager/ lighting tech, grabs the handles of the truck doors and says,

"Wait 'til you check this out!" and opens the doors.

I've seen all sorts of sets and props come out of a thousand trucks but this stuff looks amazing to me. It looks like they'd got it all from wrecking yards and rubbish tips.

The boys start undoing straps and tipping road cases onto their wheels and rolling them out as two Taragos pull up next to us. I can see Harry sitting in the passenger seat and talking excitedly to the driver, gesticulating wildly, what's left of his hair flailing as he talks. He is my favourite Australian actor and now he is walking towards me, hand outstretched, with a crazy grin on his face.

"So you must be Tony, the boys have told me all about you," tilting his head in the direction of the truck. I am smiling and looking right at him when I hear myself saying,

"It's great to meet you Harry, Welcome to our little theatre. I can hardly wait to see this show," as my smile transforms into HIS crazy grin.

He regards me for a moment, looking deep in thought. His grin has become a pensive 'staring at the ground' thing. He is wearing a medieval style shirt with frilly cuffs, open at the chest where many gold chains are hanging. His hand is resting on his chin. Abruptly he looks back up. The crazy grin is there again, and then he looks at the truck and says,

"Oh... I'm on... excuse me Tone, work to do!" and he strides off towards the truck, just as the front bench seat from an old car is wheeled out. He leaps up onto the loading dock like a 20 year old and lands on the bench seat and it slides on its wheels up against the handrail whereupon he yells,

"Oh Geoooofffrey, can I have my steering wheel please?"

He inserts the steering wheel and shaft into a lug on the bench seat's frame and clears his throat, tests the wheel as if he is about to go on a test drive.

" Ladies and gentlemen..." sounding like a barker out the front of a peep show, "Introducing, in order of their appearance on the dock, the set and props of the most amazing show you will ever see!" pushing himself around in circles, his long grey hair trailing behind him.

Old rusted oil drums, rusty barbed wire, pieces of old fences, broken service station signs, car hub caps... they all get an introduction as we unload the truck in the hazy morning light. In between announcements Harry mutters to himself, like he is rehearsing lines from a long forgotten show. I look at him and smile broadly, sensing an interesting few days ahead of me.

The Raffle
20 years ago

The next time I see him he is sitting up eating breakfast. I have just woken up from what I think was the third operation and shit, the arm is still here. He is watching me intensely. On a tray next to me are some scrambled eggs and orange juice. I pick up the eggs with my good arm and drop them 'thud' back down, then vomit loudly, narrowly missing the eggs. I go to wipe off on my arm and realise I shouldn't try to move it. I look across at him. He is grinning at me.

"What's the joke?" I scowl.

Giggling, he says: "Nothin' mate. Pete's me name."

"I'm Tony," I croak, spitting into the eggs. "That your leg there?"

"Yep. Course I got no use for it now. D'you remember waking up at all?"

"No."

"Well you were ranting about a bomb made of scrambled eggs and codeine comin' down on you! Fuck you're as crazy as everyone else here!" he says with a high-pitched laugh.

Sitting upright there is even less of him. Stringy black hair and black beard, waxy, pale skin hanging off what is left of his bones. He looks 50 but he is probably much younger. The marks of his pain are gouged deep into his face, and his eyes have that lost, faraway look. He waves his fingerless hands around when he talks. Like some demented gesture. I notice something bobbing up and down under his sheets, forgetting that lost leg in the corner. He sees me looking there.

"Yeah it does that sometimes. Looks like I'm wanking hey?"

"Shit mate, I thought you were, yeah."

We both laugh. I try to sit upright and as I do fire goes through my arm just for forgetting it. I swear heavily. The reek of my spew isn't helping either. A large nurse appears in the doorway, she is so big she blocks out all the light coming into the room. She has a needle in her hand.

"Oh Mr Cameron, look at the mess you've made!" She shakes her head and glares at me. She seems to believe I do it just to annoy her.

"Well, how can a man's vomit be expected to fit into THAT?" I grunt between pain spasms, pointing with my chin to the breakfast tray. She walks cautiously through the chuck on the floor to the table at the side of the bed. I wink at Pete.

"This is for your vomit," she says, picking up a mini bedpan. "I'll go get a mop then," looking at me disgustedly.

"Oh, um... sister... is that needle for me? Pain's really bad..."

"Uh huh... your number?"

"17659."

As she is pulling the needle out of my leg she asks me if I want to buy a ticket in the ward's Christmas raffle. She points out of the door to a Christmas tree in the corridor. My eyes follow her fat finger and see a sagging yellow pine tree with a Christmas hamper of food and a few decorations drooping off it.

Incredulously I reply, "Aah, no thanks."

The morphine is burning up my highway veins. *What fucking interest do I have in food right now?* I drift off to the swish, swish, slap, slop of a mop soaking up my aborted breakfast...

A Beach in Thailand
Present

I watch the light teasing the log as I reach across and run my hand over the scars on my arm. I feel the bump of flesh sticking out like a weird growth that came from my stomach and has been attached to my arm all these years... An overwhelming warm ball of energy rises up in my gut, floods my throat and I start to sob now and then I find myself laughing too, that laugh like when you are caught out in the rain without a coat and you surrender to it...

I feel the true horror of what I did to my arm, I look at it and it's like the wounds are still fresh and not weather beaten and tanned, not looking like a forgotten road map to nowhere in particular. The sight of my arm stripped of its skin and the glowing raw red flesh, or what was left of it, staring back at me on this beach, in this moment, mined from somewhere deep inside my patchy memories, leaping up and smiling at me 24 years later... It's all I can do to smile back...

Sledgehammer
40 years ago

I am looking all around for a place to hide as I hear a pause in the destruction of the kitchen. I tense up and close my mouth tight, look at Nadia who looks right back at me with the same terror in her eyes and then she is talking on the phone.

"Yes, yes that's right Nadia Swallow. He's wrecking everything, come quick! 14 Daours Court... please hurry!"

She puts the phone down and puts a finger to her lips and whispers,

"Ssshh, I'll get you out of here."

My bottom lip is trembling when I see the tears on her cheeks. The smashing has resumed with a mighty roar from my father's mouth and with each heavy thud Nadia jumps in her skin.

I stand still.

The thuds seem dull and distant to me. I do not flinch. Across from me, one of the bedroom doors opens and my brother is standing there, eyes bulging. As he starts to move towards me, a massive crash comes from the kitchen, followed by the clinking of bottles... the fridge! Nadia reaches out to grab my brother as he enters through the open glass doors, he instinctively brushes her arm out of the way like he does on the football ground and heads straight for me... he picks me up and turns around to get out when we both hear Nadia's voice yelling at him,

"Craig! Give him to me and go find your Mum. I think she's with your sister!"

Upon hearing that, he stops and looks at her for a moment, puts me back down and runs out of the room, changing direction in one swift movement...

Liquid Moments
16 years ago

"What are we gonna do today, Daddy?" Han asks through a mouthful of cornflakes, "can we go on an adventure?"

"Yeah, an adventure Dad!" Cass chimes in.

"Weeelllll, leeets see…"

I put a finger to my chin in mock thought and smile at my girls, whose eyes light up when they see the cheeky side coming out in me. I listen to the rain beating down hard on the tin roof of the house and say,

"It's a bit wet out there, I don't know…" sounding dubious.

"Oh Dad, C'MON!"

I think for a while.

"OK, how about this? Let's write an adventure story together and that way we won't get wet!"

"YAY!" they shriek in unison, and start shovelling in the cornflakes so they can get started.

"OK," I say, "but this time you two make it up and I'll just write it down, what do you think? What will we write? Will it be a fun story, a scary story? What?"

"A scary AND a funny story" Cass says sensibly.

I rustle through the debris on the kitchen table and uncover a notepad and a pen. I start to write 'Cass and Hannah's Adventure Story' at the top of the page when Han shouts,

"I know, I know! It's about a father and daughter who go into a scary forest and they get, like, scared and that!"

She is tapping her hands on the table to a beat in her head when I look up at her. I return to the page and write:

'An oak forest in autumn... a father and his daughter are walking along a path covered in leaves...'

" So what are they doing there Han?" I inquire.

"Uummm, lets see... um, they're going to pile up all the leaves and run and jump into the piles."

"Is it cold? What are they wearing?" I ask, taking a sip of my coffee and eyeing off the coffee machine on the stove.

"Yep, it's really cold," she replies," and windy too, Dad, it's like blowing all the trees around and making all the leaves fly around."

"Awesome!" I exclaim, and continue writing...

'He pulls up his coat collar and blows on his bare hands as he watches...'

"What's her name Cass?" I ask.

"Umm... I think her name should be Pearl."

'...Pearl leaping into the pile of leaves, a pile of leaves twice her height before she sprays them everywhere, shrieking with laughter. Suddenly a gust of wind hits the forest and all they can hear is the whoosh of the wind in the trees and the creaking of the branches as they strain under the gusts of wind...'

Han, speaking quickly, says "And the wind gets really strong and blows them over. And then they get lost!"

"Oh dear, I hope they can get out of there," I say with a concerned look.

"Well that's the thing Dad, they keep trying to leave but the wind stops them and then they have to stay the night!"

I gaze at my 4-year old daughter, a gaze full of wonder.

I write feverishly as she says, "Luckily, the Dad has some matches and a Mars bar so they start a fire and eat the Mars bars and then they went to sleep!"

"Boy, must've been a cold night's sleep!"

"Yeah Dad, freezing! But she hops into her Dad's coat and cuddles up and they keep each other warm." Cass doesn't even look up from her drawing when she says this.

"OK, so they wake up in the morning and what happens?" my pen poised above the page.

"Um," Han almost sighs, "Well, they try and get out of the forest again but the wind is still too strong. Every time they reach the edge of the forest the wind pushes them back... They're like trapped, Dad, and they can't get out!"

"Shit, Han, it's gettin' a bit scary now," as I write...

The wind howls and the trees moan, almost like a ghost talking to them, laughing at them... '

"But it's OK Dad, because Pearl realises it isn't the forest that has stopped them leaving at all!"

"Oh really?"

"Yeah, cause it's the story that has trapped them Dad, they are trapped in this story..."

I look up at her, still drumming on the table, and I smile adoringly at her and say,

"But how do we get them out?"

The Raffle
20 years ago

I watch a movie in my head.

I am high above an operating room as a man is being wheeled in. He is laughing maniacally as they try to restrain him. There is the sound of crows squawking nearby. He looks out of the window and he can see the hospital's incinerator belching smoke, crows circling the chimney and beyond that the orange/brown hazy city. Down there people are going to work, Uni, they are shopping, eating, fucking... Down there people are like ghosts inhabiting a life; present, but not really there at all. He laughs again.

How ironic, I think, *up here with one of the best views around and I am having dead flesh scraped off me whilst the living dead go through the motions below me.*

A man in a mask and gloves appears.

"Morning Tone, up for another visit I see, boy, there'll be nothing left of you soon, haha!"

That's funny, I think, *he has the same name as me...*

"OK mate, just count back from 100..."

The anaesthetist looks at the bewildered expression on my face and says,

"Sorry mate, just a bit of surgery humour..."

And I think, *One day I am going to make it to 90.*

And as I drift into unconsciousness I can hear trolleys being pushed into position around me.

"Poor bastard." I hear one of them say.

The Release
5 years ago

I sit on my bed and try to write as the first sun comes through my window. She is coming to get the last of her stuff today and I am not ready for this moment. I have been up since 4a.m trying to write a goodbye letter to her: words on a page uninterrupted by arguments, some way of making it right between us... and failing. I have smoked heavily and drank way too much coffee already and at dawn I am jittery and my head hurts.

I go downstairs to put more wood on the fire and later I see myself standing in front of the fire having got lost in memories of my children running excitedly around their new house and their Mum arranging flowers in a vase in the kitchen, dogs sleeping on couches... and much later I picture my lover languishing half naked on the couch on one of those summer days that feels like the world is coming to an end, the bush tinder dry around us, the wind a hot thief straight off the desert, robbing the day of reason.

And finally the words come, they rush through my head and I struggle to keep astride of them as I write. Two hours later, I sit back on the couch feeling wrung out entirely and also strangely rejuvenated. I can hear car tyres on the gravel on my driveway... Shit, she is here!

She looks stressed when she walks in, and I can't help but watch her long legs walking towards me in tight Levis.

I smile at her, a wounded smile. She smiles back at me the same way. We are both wounded and we just want it over with, this day, this final moment when the last of her stuff, the last of her, leaves my house, leaves my life.

I hold my hand out with the letter in it and I hear myself saying, as if from miles away,

"This is for you Lisa."

She takes it and says, "Thanks", in a neutral way. Then, "Well, I better get into it I s'pose..."

"Yeah I guess so..."

***

It doesn't seem long before she is gone. I hear the gravel being squished under her tyres as she turns out of the driveway and onto the dirt road. For quite a while I am silent. For the first time since I had built this house I am alone. No children, no dogs, no partner, no photos on the wall... every room except the lounge is empty. Even the great acoustic can't disguise the emptiness. My footsteps echo through the place.

"No photos on the wall" I mutter to myself.

Within minutes I am starting the Duke and collecting helmet, jacket, gloves, boots and some cash and backing out the door, taking one last look at the place.

No photos on the wall.

The Ducati is idling and purring like a tiger as I fasten my helmet and give my gloves one final stretch. I roll her off the centre -stand and look across at this dream I used to have. A home for my family, a

34

sustainable solar powered sculptural thing that had sprung out of my imagination some 12 years before. I rev the engine a touch and on the downward revs put her in gear and then all I can hear is the squish of the gravel and the rumbling tiger underneath me.

I ease the bike through the gears and cruise the 4kms into Newstead at 80 km/hr.

Good for old bikes, take them slowly, let 'em warm up and then go for it...

And this Ducati had never missed a beat in the 11 years I had owned it. The old girl was coming up for 30 years old; older, I mused, than my last girlfriend had been.

How the fuck did this happen? How did I not see the signs? Did I just stop seeing altogether? No photos on the fucking wall, man, how did it get to that?

Leaving Newstead, I take her to redline in every gear and she is growling now as I fly over the Moloort plains at 160km/hr, the howling staccato rhythm punctuating my thoughts. The bike is running like a dream and I lie on it and duck my head beneath the half-fairing just like Agostini. My head is being buffeted by the speed and my knees are squeezing the tank, my hands locked around the handgrips. I am pulling out to pass cars at least 100 metres before I get to them. I can see the straight road I am on start winding into some small hills, and a small car between those hills and me.

I HAVE to get past that car so it doesn't fuck up the corners for me.

So I squeeze as much as I can get out of the Duke and make a run for it. A second or so later I realise that I have miscalculated the move and I find myself passing the car mid-corner at 140km/hr. It is then that I see the shadow of a large truck approaching me, followed by the truck itself. I squeeze through the gap with a handful of milliseconds to spare. Horns are blaring behind me as I huddle back down under the fairing and open her up again, my teeth clenched and a grimace on my face.

High-speed chess, Tone, high-speed chess...

An hour or so later I am at Dunkeld, some 150kms from home, at the southern end of the Grampians National Park. I have heard there is a good road that runs through the guts of it, surrounded by rugged mountains and untouched forest. I stop to fuel up, feeling like I have just ridden for 10 hours.

My 39 year-old body is stiff despite the yoga and I struggle to get my leg over the bike. Once I am back on, I feel all right again. The motor is red hot and starts with a wilful grin, as if saying,

'Is that it? That all you got old fella?'

No photos on the wall.

My face relaxes the grimace it has been wearing and a smile spreads slowly across it as I drop her gently into first gear...

The road is better than I thought, a wet dream for a motorcyclist, and even though the bike is willing to go to redline again I am not. A strange calm has passed over me, the speedo says 120km/hr but it feels like it is in slow-mo. The trees next to the road are magnificent specimens towering over the road, the sun dappled by the canopy and sending shafts of light to the ground through which I ride. I slow down to 80km/hr and open the face visor and smell the scent of eucalypts and let my face get bathed in the shafts of light. I look down and see my hands letting go of the handlebars and then they are stretched high above my head. I tilt my head back and close my eyes and float down a gentle hill to the bottom of the ancient valley...

A Desert and a Slide Guitar
4 years ago

The stage manager gives the beginners call and all the actors make their way to their entrance positions in various parts of the wings. I am being told from Front of House, *'The house is in, the house is in, Tony you have clearance'* over the two way radio jammed against my ear as Harry strides over to me. He is wearing a pair of stubby shorts, a short sleeve shirt and an old tattered sunhat, all pretty dirty. I hold my hand up to him and tilt my head down and talk to the stage manager through the talkback system.

"You have clearance, Bek, the house is yours." Harry is still standing there when I look up.

"Hey, Harry, break a leg man."

"Thanks Tone. Hey listen, do you know of any good bookshops in this town? I wanna check some out tomorrow, after the matinee."

"Matter of fact I do, there are a few good ones... The best is opposite the park, near the brothel... I could show you if you want?"

"I was hoping you'd say that... OK gotta go, I'm on, gotta go, I'm on..."

He walks over to the edge of stage against one of the curtain legs that mask the backstage from the audience, gives me a wink and looks out at the stage.

I can see it through the curtains, a shaft of artifice, a glimpse of unreality as I sit in blue light and watch Harry make his entrance as a tired old newsagent from the middle of nowhere. The props look amazing lit on the stage, the plush velvet of the house curtains a strange counterpoint to the junkyard desert scene Harry walks into.

I get up quietly and walk around the very back of the stage in the dark and as I pass each curtain leg I can hear 'Bazza', Harry's character, attempting to seduce his girlfriend and failing.

"For Christ's sake, Bazza, we're too old for that stuff now, you gotta find another hobby..."

"A hobby?" Bazza then waxes lyrically like a wounded poet, full of Aussie slang but beautiful in its own way. I am standing next to one of the French braces that are holding up the wall of his 'house' and looking at a man totally immersed in the moment. He has transformed himself; he IS Bazza.

I walk slowly back to the SM position and when I get there Bazza is walking off stage towards Bek and me, holding his gut and limping. He holds the walk and the lost bewildered expression until he is past the curtains, stops abruptly and then does John Cleese's silly walk, pulling his hair up and out and shaking his head from side to side.

He stops the antics when he gets to me. Bek is smiling and shaking her head in mock disapproval. I am holding my mouth to stop laughing loudly.

"So anyway mate, tomorrow... you up for it?" he whispers.

"I was hoping you'd say that." I say, grinning at him.

A Beach in Thailand
Present

The log is rolling in the water, almost submerging as each wave passes, sliding down its back and sinking for just a moment. I see my arms clasped tight around it, I see me struggling for breath, I see myself scanning the immediate horizon for another set of monster waves to leap up out of the angry monsoon soup. Beyond the break I can see plastic, a lot of plastic... and more logs and brightly coloured broken pieces of boats. It's like they have formed a rough queue and are awaiting their ride to the beach, their final resting place.

I can hear the muffled roar of another plane taking off below the thundering hiss of the waves crashing and insinuating themselves on the beach, coming closer to me with each set. I can feel the sand sinking under my weight as it prepares to give itself back to the ocean. My eyes are blurry when I look away from the log. My body is quivering with the raw emotions pouring through it.

Fuck, I guess everyone has a trigger, I think, *something that sets them off... Am I going mad or am I merely becoming aware of my madness for the first time? Shit, I haven't cried and laughed this much in my entire life... what the fuck is happening to me?*

The Raffle
20 years ago

I wake up with a start. I am surrounded by blurry white figures. I blink, but I can't seem to focus on them. One is saying,

"Yes, well we better book him in ASAP so we can remove... aaah, Mr Cameron, good morning..."

My eyes are clearing.

"I'm afraid there is more necrotic tissue which we'll have to remove in order to save your arm..."

He is, no... all nine or ten of them are looking at my arm. It has turned black again.

He turns to his interns,

"This is the worst crush injury I've seen in a long while. Both bones and arteries crushed, reconnected 12 hours after the accident, several debridements, vein grafts, muscle grafts..." then turning to me he asks, "You're not a concert pianist, are you, Mr Cameron?"

I look at him with contempt as a smile appears at the corners of his mouth. "Because that would be a real tragedy, would it not?"

Flicking through my file, he then says, "Aah, here it is, a labourer, well that's alright then."

The interns look embarrassingly at their feet through the silence that follows. I glare at the overfed reddening face of the surgeon and say,

"Gees, I was thinking that it'd be nice to be able to hold my children up above my head, dress myself, stuff like that, you fucking prick!"

I spit on the floor at his feet as he says,

"Um, so we'll see you upstairs in the operating room tomorrow morning," as if we had just made a play date.

He moves off towards Pete and the rest follow. Out the window Melbourne's brown sludge air has thinned a bit so everything has a brown/ orange tinge to it. Blue/ orange crows fly over to brown/ orange trees. The doctor gods are now with the man next to me, Alf, and he is busy telling them the complete history of his illness, whatever it is.

"So when's your next one?" It is Pete.

"Tomorrow. Got to scrape more rotting flesh off me. How about you?"

"Nah, still not strong enough to take the anaesthetic. Fuck 'em; if I can drink five litres of wine a day then I can handle five hours surgery. Aah, me hips buggered, mate, the bone's like broken glass, and me right knee's gotta come off...

He stares off down the hall.

"How long did ya keep that up?" I ask, meaning the drinking.

"Seven, maybe eight years. Dunno anymore."

"Uh huh."

Liquid Moments
14 years ago

Three more whacks with the hammer, I say to myself, as my mangled arm brings it down on the nail. *OK, two more...* My hand has cramped and the last two fingers cannot be convinced to grab the handle. My corkscrewed lower arm bones ache right where the car roof had hit it all those years ago as I drive the nail home, the last of hundreds Dave and I have driven into the rafters today.

After two months of making pisé walls I finally got to roof height. Shovelling mud, then constructing three forms a day and pouring them has turned to standing on a plank at 5 metres and nailing rafters into place. At least the view is spectacular from up here. I can see down past the highway to the river; the whole valley spread out before me and alive with the sound of birds... and my growls of pain as my arm reaches the end of its tether for the day. My mate Dave has downed tools, climbed down his ladder and says to me,

"Well that's it for me, I'm buggered, and I don't want to listen to your wails of pain anymore! Jesus, take it easy on yourself, that's a pretty serious injury you've got there!"

As he talks, I am watching the dogs trot happily down the driveway and take a left onto the dirt road. Soon they are galloping towards my girls as they come over the hill back from school, their tails wagging wildly from side to side.

"Thanks for the help today buddy, but not for the pity. I'll be right. See ya tomorrow?"

I hook my thumb into my shirt collar, a sling of sorts and back myself down the 5 metres of extension ladder, holding on with my shins and my left arm...

"Yep, bout 10. Alright, catch ya Tone..."

I sit, exhausted, with my back against a wall that wasn't there last week as Hannah whizzes around the house site on a little step-through motorbike. Cass sits next to me, she sees me grimace with pain.

"Daddy, can I ask you something?"

"Sure, sweetie."

"How come you are building our house when you have a sore arm? Can't we pay someone so you can rest your arm?"

I smile at her.

"It's something I've always wanted to do and I'm really getting into it, Cass. I love it!"

"And Dad, how come you have put someone else's old windows and doors into our new house, and how come it's not like my friend's houses?"

I watch Hannah zoom past, fly over one of the mounds of dirt we made for a jump, and go straight over the handlebars when she lands. She bounces back up and looks at the bike on its side with the back wheel still turning.

"Well Cass, I guess it's because your Dad is a little different to your friend's dads..."

"But why, Dad? Why build it when your arm is sore every night?"

Then it came to me, how to say it.

"I am not building this house, Cass." I pause to look at her, "This house is building me…"

Sledgehammer
40 years ago

One of the kitchen chairs flies through the door and slides into the dining room table, breaking on impact. Nadia screams and lifts me up onto her bony hip and starts for the front door. I turn around and see the same hairy hand holding a sledgehammer by the neck; I see the insane rage in my father's eyes… He is looking at me looking at him when he yells,

"And you better get the fuck out of my way!"

He smiles madly at me as he raises the sledgehammer and brings it down hard on the crystal display cabinet. Nadia stands there trembling. The cabinet withstands the first blow but not the next one, which smashes the top, or the next and the next, until there are shards of crystal flying everywhere…

Nadia turns and runs for the front door. I haven't taken my eyes off my father, and now there is a fierceness in my gaze. I am kicking and punching Nadia with my 4 year-old fists so that she will let me go, but she hangs on tight.

Just then, my Mum comes around the corner of the corridor to the bedrooms clutching my two-year old sister, who is screaming so much her whole body is bright red. My brother is holding my Mum's hand with this strange bewildered look on his face. My Mum is totally freaked and shudders as she hears the crystal cabinet being destroyed.

"Quick Nadia, get him out of here!"

The Release
3 years ago

I am standing on the steps of the County court, heart quietly pounding, drinking coffee and wondering where to put my cigarette butt. I am waiting. Waiting to meet my barrister, waiting for this moment to go away, this whole day to disappear like those dreams you never remember after you have woken up. I am wearing my funeral/ court suit I had tailor-made for $40 in Vietnam whilst on a holiday with the woman who will be in that court room in 15 minutes: a woman whom I loved, but didn't really get it until she was gone. By then it was a broken thing, like the shards of crystal flying across my childhood memories. I wriggle uncomfortably in my suit; I yank at the tie and shrug my shoulders as if I'm convincing it to feel right. But it doesn't, it just doesn't. This whole day doesn't...

I feel numb and disconnected from everything around me. The tram that passes doesn't seem to be making any noise, but I hear the barista frothing milk 10 metres away like it is a jackhammer right next to me... *c'mon man,* I say to myself, *keep it together... try and focus on the bed of lies her case sits on.*

I see myself on the Moolort plains on my bike passing that car, and it seems like a lifetime ago. It seems like something to hold on to, today, of all days... I finish the last of my coffee as a young man approaches me.

"Tony Cameron?"

"Aah yeah, you must be my barrister then?"

"Indeed I am." He holds out his hand and I take it, give him the mangled right hand.

He can't be more than 28, fuck!

"Call me Marty. Well, we better get up there. Nice suit by the way!"

I walk up the steps with him in my $40 suit and notice the cut and quality of his - probably worth more than my car - as we walk into the all-too-familiar foyer and head to the security check point...

***

Afterwards, I walk aimlessly around the CBD without a clue where I am going. And I don't care either. The woman who *promised* my mother and my children that she would never take me to court for money if we split up, has just done that. The woman who I allowed to live in my house for free for 4 years...

The house I had built for my family was now on the table and she wanted a share. When I had split with the girls' Mum, it had been fair and we had split things evenly.

I remember walking down the same courthouse steps just 6 years ago and into the arms of this same woman who had just lied through her teeth for the last 3 hours.

How the fuck did I get here? What happened? Where the fuck did I go wrong?

And then I understood. I had coached her in how to take me to court, for fuck's sake. She was there 'supporting' me the last time I was here. Every move she made, she knew would get to me. And it did.

All around me, jackets fly open and ties wrap themselves around necks as gusts of wind blow between the skyscrapers. Women's neat hair is being buffeted and messed with, and those business-like expressions on the featureless faces contort into caricatures of themselves.

I start laughing as I walk; imagining the clothes actually peeling off them and being blown into the gutters. Men are left standing in their business socks and shoes and underwear. Those who had opted to free-ball were paying for it now, and I laugh again as I watch briefcases being frantically thrust in front of their bare and dangling genitalia. It is harder for the women, of course, and I see some of them frozen in thought, 'The boobs or the pussy?' as they struggle with handbags and anything else they can find to cover themselves up. I even see one fishing through a garbage bin and coming out with a plastic bag and fashioning it into a makeshift bra, a self satisfied look on her face.

I look down at my body. *How long have I been naked? I can't even remember my clothes coming off.*

And suddenly the wind stops and an eerie silence descends on the street. Now it isn't just me laughing. I can hear guffaws and snickers, chortles and giggles turning slowly into raucous belly bursting laughter. Soon enough those around me are bellowing with such intensity, an almost mocking intensity, that it sends a chill through me.

I can hear the eerie sound of a musical saw and an organ, the intro to an Eels song, slow and ponderous.

> *'I'm gonna tell you what you need to hear*
> *And I'm a little too late*
> *By three or four years*

And it may not make much sense
Now that we are apart
But I'm gonna stop pretending
That I didn't break your heart'

I can hear the semi-acoustic electric guitar plucking away through the solo just as I pass a CD store, a place called Discurio. I see my naked self in the reflection. I have a hunted look on my face. Beyond the glass is a poster for a Miles Davis CD. I walk on in.

Some time later I am slowly going through the jazz CD's, looking for "Nerfititi" by Miles and sure enough I find it. Just then my phone rings. I look at the caller ID and there isn't one. *Phew*, I think, *I don't wanna talk to anyone I know about my day right now.*

So I answer.

"Hi Tony, it's Michelle here. From '*Nightcafe*', we came through your venue in May. How are you?"

Through the haze of six months worth of shows, I struggle to see her face.

"I'm great Michelle, and you?"

I am buying time so I can remember her… and then I see the stick, her walking stick, and her tiny face now, a petite dancer's face.

"I'm great, thanks… Hey, I was wondering, I'm in Melbourne over the next few days, you know, visiting friends, having more tests, and I was hoping we might be able to catch up while I'm here, have a few drinks. You got time to come down?"

I remember a drunken night with her and her troupe in an apartment after a great show doing vodka shooters until we all passed out around the place.

"I'm in Melbourne now, as a matter of fact. Where are you?"

Perfect, she doesn't know anything about this shit I'm stuck in...

A Desert and a Slide Guitar
4 years ago

    I have been up in the lighting grid watching the show, my favourite spot in the theatre. Up there, I can see the beads of sweat rolling down the backs of the necks of the actors, as the stage lights they obsessively desire slowly cook them. Up there, I can see the lights going on and off, changing colour, I can hear the loud buzz of the 108 lighting dimmers working hard just next to me. A shit-load of electricity just a metre from me. The lights are hidden from the audience, the actors simply being lit from nowhere, as if by magic. Up there I can see into the flys; all the ropes and pulleys that are holding up the tonnes of lights and scenic cloths above the actors' heads, I can see the back of the set with actors behind them quickly doing a costume change or a make-up touch up. I can smell the sweat rising up with the heat of the lights.

    Now I am side of stage in blue light just behind the house curtain on OP opposite Bek, crouched down catching my breath as 'Bazza' continues his desert road trip. I hear him talking to the German backpacker he has picked up hitchhiking, and I can see them through the gap in the curtains. Down here side of stage, crouched down just out of the coverage of the stage lights, it is different, but just as fascinating to me. From here I can see where the make-up line ends on their faces and more beads of sweat, this time dripping down past their ears.

Bazza yells: "Look out!" and swerves as an imaginary kangaroo hops onto their path.

He sighs disgustedly… "Fuckin' roos!" Then there is a pause.

"Yeah I used to know where I was going too, when I was young like you… I used to like what I saw in the mirror just like you would…" he trails off as his gaze leaves the 'road' and wanders up and down the girl's body.

He pauses, turns to the audience and gives them a big wink. They burst out laughing which I can see eggs Bazza on. He puts a hand to the side of his mouth, as if whispering to the audience.

"In two scenes I will be dead, why the hell not?"

Which leads to more laughter from the crowd. I look across stage and watch Bek frantically searching through her script and then smile as the realisation hits her that he is just improvising. She returns to her knitting.

"Now I don't know which road I'm on or why… and everyone else's fuckin' headlights are blasting me as they drive in the opposite direction…"

He turns to the girl and says…"It's like this, Helga" and reaches toward an imaginary dashboard and suddenly the stage is plunged into darkness. You can hear her scream and Bazza laughing over a soundtrack of everyday life, traffic, busy shopping malls, the ching of a cash register, the roar of a football crowd, the squeal of car tyres, grating metal…

There is a single tight circle of white light on Bazza's face.

"You can't see the road at all… there are signs all over the place urging you to turn off at the next off ramp but the off ramps are going nowhere as well. Into a slow death in suburbia, surrounded by products that 'define your individuality'..."

The lone white light is joined by a cool, madhouse blue that washes the stage around them.

"You start your mower at 10a.m on a Sunday like everyone else, you watch 'A Current fuckin' Affair' and start to believe the shit they are telling you and then, well, you might as well be dead Helga... that's just death on the instalment plan, you read Celine, Helga?"

"Turn ze lights on please!" she pleads.

He ignores her and continues with his rant, it slowly decreasing in sense as the look of alarm increases on Helga's face and the cool madhouse blue fades slowly to black...

***

Afterwards, Harry and I are walking through the park on our way to the bookshop. A lot of the students that have clustered in the park from the nearby school are staring at Harry and giggling. He is wearing the same medieval shirt as before and now wears a three quarter coat with renaissance cuffs and old boots like a pirate's, with his thin grey hair flying behind him as we talk about our favourite writers. The talk is exciting us both, as we sense a kindred spirit, someone with fire in their eyes and a hunger for knowledge that only rests in sleep...

And my kindred spirit looks like a cross between a pirate, Einstein and the ringmaster from a broken down circus...

Harry's eyes are bulging when we walk into the second hand bookshop. He looks up at the two levels of books and prepares to immerse himself in it with a few Yoga style breaths.

***

On the way back to the theatre he talks excitedly about his purchases, they are good, if not great, reads. Classics, from Genet to Burroughs via Kerouac, Byron, Conrad, Brecht, Miller, Bukowski… He starts reading passages to me on the way to the theatre, and I tell him a little bit about my life.

"But Tony, I don't get it, how did you end up here?"

"What d'ya mean?"

"Well you're alive, what the fuck are you doing in this backwater? You could be anywhere in the world doing all sorts of things, why here for fuck's sake?"

I mumble stuff about raising a family, building an earth home, but it sounds weak, even to me.

"Oh bullshit, Tone, you're hiding, that's what you you're doing!"

Defensive now, I ask, "Hiding from what, you fucking lunatic?"

He puts his hand on my shoulder like a father would to his son and says,

"From yourself, brother, from yourself…"

A Beach in Thailand
Present

'Sorry Harry, haven't got there yet' I stutter between what seems to be relentless sobbing as I stare at my log, the only thing my eyes will focus on right now, the only thing in my world right now. The waves determinedly attempt to toss it onto the beach but the log wants nothing of it, lolling about unperturbed by the commotion going on around it.

The log seems to be teasing the ocean somehow and it makes me think of Lisa leaning against the stairway, wet and glistening from the shower, naked, deep red ringlets on her bare shoulders.

I hear her saying, "I'm all wet baby, I think I might go upstairs and… aah… dry myself…"

A twisted grin pushes its way through my tears and my log rolls like a baby seal playing… I can feel a huge ball of dead weight moving restlessly inside me…

The Raffle
20 years ago

When I wake from the operation I find myself in a different bed in a different room. A small room. For one. Miraculously my arm is still there, now stitched onto my stomach.

This time, they have cut an 8-inch square flap of skin, fat and muscle, opened it up, put my arm inside and then sewed it back up. Every time I went upstairs, less of me came back. They had tried everything. They had taken bits of my leg, bum and gut and tried to get them to 'take' onto my arm, to cover the bone, because everything else had rotted away. This was the last resort.

To me, my arm looks like a Sunday roast the day after. My visitors don't seem to get the joke...

A nurse comes in and tells me I have been put in isolation. A small problem of an infectious staph I had picked up in one of the hospitals I had been screaming and swearing in. She is wearing a mask, gown and gloves. I look around the room; I can see the TV on a trolley and a small table over in one corner. The nurse walks across to the window, opens the curtains and bright light pours into the room. Once my eyes have adjusted I look out the window. I have a view of a brick wall. Slowly I begin to feel my body under the sheets. My legs feel tiny, like they have sunken into the bed somehow and my feet are numb.

My eyes struggle to focus on anything. A dull throb like a blacksmith warming up shoots through my arm and I scream through a grimace which sends the nurse scurrying out of the room and returning with another syringe of morphine.

The throbbing becomes a distant thing. I look out the window at the brick wall and start counting. I pull out the Walkman my friend Totto had given me with the lapel microphone, hit record then hear myself saying,

'OK, stir-crazy hospital ramblings chapter 2... isolation...' in a sluggish, groggy and dreamy way...

The Release
3 years ago

I have changed out of my suit and I am walking down Flinders Lane feeling freer than I have in years. 'Mojitos Bar' is around here somewhere, and as I walk my eyes dart back and forth whilst my legs are listening to Mile's *Nerfititi*. They have some sort of loose, funky yet jerky thing going on.

Two years of not being able to work on finishing my house has just about done me in. I have had my dream held up to my face and placed just out of reach... The more I had improved the place, the more money Lisa would have gotten, since everything I needed to do would have added value to the house. I was on first name terms with her property valuer, having had the experience of him visiting me several times over the last 7 years, the first visit due to the first split, with Em. He reckoned I had the most valued property in the area. Six valuations in 7 years, fuck, I had probably bought him golf clubs several times over.

Flinders Lane is being its run-down, swanky, cool self as my liquid legs send me down a small laneway off to the left, past cool little shoe shops with insanely expensive shoes and staff with so much attitude you were lucky if they even acknowledged you were there. I see a man gingerly reaching for a pair of shoes when, like lightning, the heavily pierced sales girl pounces on him.

"What the fuck are you doing, SIR?" through grinding teeth and suddenly I am thinking of the movie 'Repo Man' from the 80's, where the punk couple have just robbed a liquor store and killed everyone inside, and afterward, outside, catching their breath, the punk guy says, "OK, let's go get sushi... and not pay!"

I see a bar ahead spread on either side of the laneway. When I am in the middle of it I stop and look around, and there she is, long black hair and red lipstick smile. I am beaming when I walk towards her. She is much smaller than before, shit, most dancers are lucky to weigh 40 kilos at best and Michelle looks drawn, her face wearing a sunken look through the smile as I sit down opposite.

"I am so glad you called, Michelle."

"Me too. So how are you?"

I thought about it for a while. "You know Michelle, I'm feeling fucking great!"

"Well, order one of these," sipping her cocktail, "and you will feel positively fan-fucking-tastic!" She winks and then laughs a loud raucous laugh that seems totally incongruous coming out of the petite woman in front of me.

"So, how's Melbourne treating you?" I inquire.

"Oh it's great, I love these laneways full of quirky stuff, it's so European..."

She puts a hand on her walking stick, which is hooked over the edge of the table, as she says, "but I get tired of walking pretty quickly, and it's a great city to walk through..."

"Yeah it's a pity we don't have cyclos like in Vietnam, they could ride you around all day..."

"And get me a massage too!" she chirps, laughing.

"So, how's Melbourne treating *you*?" she asks me.

"It's been one of the most bizarre days of my life, and it's getting better and better as the day progresses."

"Salutee!" she holds up her glass.

We down our drinks, look at each other for a second or two, then I turn my gaze to a passing waiter.

"Two more please," then turning to Michelle, "Let's have a proper go at this drinking business, what d'ya say?"

"I'm a dancer, it's my job," she declares. I look at the stick. The night has begun.

Several drinks later, I say, "Michelle, can I tell you something?"

"Yep, sure!"

"I think I am having what they call a cathartic moment and I just wanted to say I can't think of anyone better to see it out with..."

"Oh really, everything OK?"

"Yeah, everything's OK," a smile wells up inside of me, "right now, right here in this moment..."

She looks at me and raises a theatrical eyebrow, "Oh, really?"

***

We are walking out of the small laneway. We walk slowly, and often she loses her balance and grabs onto my arm. She has a bony desperateness to her, and I wonder how many times this once lithe woman has fallen to the ground with no-one to help her, how many times she has wistfully watched her dancers do things she used to be able to do.

We haven't mentioned the MS eating away at her nervous system and I decide not to bring it up right there and then. She stops at the corner to catch her breath and steady herself. She turns to me and asks, "Would you like to see a movie I made?"

"Sure."

She hails a cab. "My hotel is just around the corner, shouldn't take long and then we can head out for more cocktails. Sound good?"

"Sounds perfect Michelle."

Back at her room we are sitting on her couch with a laptop on the glass coffee table. She looks at me and smiles, turns to the laptop and says,

"OK, this is my story..."

She clicks the play icon and I find myself looking at some black and white abstract shapes, the camera starts moving as a cello is plucked rhythmically, with a skeletal sound to it. It pans down what appears to be a woman's body lying on her side, in extreme close up, the cello starts missing beats and losing its rhythm and then finding it again as the camera pans down past her hip bone, past the tiny curve of her waist and down her leg.

There is a slow fade to Michelle sitting backwards on a bentwood chair, on a stage. Colour images of some wild contemporary dance are being projected onto her body. She is staring at the camera, her face ablaze with projected light. The cello has been joined by an upright bass, a viola and a violin. The stuttering rhythmic pulse builds and starts getting messy and intense, almost angry. Her tiny hands form fists and she raises them straight out to the sides.

Cut to her staggering along a beach, lots of hand held shots of her legs, then her face, then a medium shot from in front, then a revolving 360 degree shot around her. The music is determined, chunky sounding and has a firm hold on the pulse... The music stops as she falls to the ground, shot from 6 different angles, one fall becoming six...

You can hear the sound of seagulls and children playing, the squeak of a swing being played on and the eerie reverb-laden breathing of Michelle lying in the sand. Cut to her sliding along a huge steel sculpture shaped like a sperm whale, she slides gracefully as the music starts to build again, this time with a sweet melancholic sound coming from the violin. She is watching the girls on the swings from a pier and the images look like 1960's technicolour.

Cut to her walking on the pier, teetering with each step, the camera a point of view shot, as if she has the camera strapped to her head. The music is soft and mellow, a counterpoint to her stumbling gait. Cut to seagulls flying gracefully across the water, the violinist playing all these upper harmonics that brings a tear to my eye.

Cut back to Michelle; close up of her face watching the seagulls fly away... Fade to black, the music slowly fades out and this is followed by a series of still photos of Michelle with her dance troupe, stick in hand in a rehearsal space, talking to them, of her sitting and watching her choreography come to life. The credits roll over them...

It is a while before either of us say anything.

"So, what do you think?"

I turn and look at her. I feel totally humbled by her story.

"That was the most beautiful thing Michelle, a poetic and poignant story. Thank you so much for showing me this today."

I pause, deep in thought, then say, "I feel like I was meant to see you today of all days... can't explain it, but I just feel it, y'know?"

"Well, lets go party then!" she shrieks.

Out on the street she starts to hail a cab and I stop her, saying, "I've got an idea... Can I be your legs tonight?"

"What do you mean?"

"Let me show you," and I stand in front of her and crouch down, "OK, on you go, jump on!"

She squeals with laughter as she climbs onto my back. I wrap my arms under her knees and we both set off up the street in search of more cocktails, and laughing into the cool Melbourne night...

Sledgehammer
40 years ago

The front door flies open and Nadia goes through it quickly with me in her arms. I feel for the last of the three bumps that means we are down the steps whilst looking back at the house, waiting for the sight of my brother, sister and mother coming out after us. But they do not. I am hanging over Nadia's shoulder, trying to crawl up and leap off and go back into the house but she feels this and tightens her grip. Just then, I see the TV go flying through the lounge room window and land in the front yard, exploding on impact, the channel knob narrowly missing our heads as it flies past. A crazy laughter is coming from the house, Nadia is staggering in the dark, weaving down the driveway, half bent over, with her free hand out in front of her like she is blind...

Now everything in the lounge room is being launched out the front window, I can hear it smashing into the garden beds and onto the street. Nadia finally straightens up and puts her hand to her side. I can hear my Mum inside the house screaming, "Stop it! Stop it!" and I can also hear my sister howling.

I look around now, I see the neighbours out in the street, the Rowes, the Sampsons. The Thompsons from next door are in their pyjamas and are looking at the consumer goods landing in pieces all around them and listening in horror to the insane laughter coming from my father's mouth as he stands at the broken window surveying his carnage. He is silhouetted by the light behind him, it turns his face into a black pool through which only the whites of his eyes penetrate. Where are my brother and sister?

Nadia is running down the driveway now and it is when we hit the pavement that I see a car parked outside my house. A white car, just like ours. With someone in it...

<u>Liquid Moments</u>
14 years ago

It's after dark by the time I get to the clean-up after the day's work, and my arm is aching. The lime from the render is eating into my hands and turning every cut into stinging craters as I run a wet brush of water around the edges where the timber doorframe meets the wall. Miles Davis is blowing a twisted solo.

It's all about the edges, I mutter to myself as I reveal the red timber that has been covered in cement, sand and lime all day. The timing is critical with this stuff: if it is too wet, the wall finish looks amateurish, lumpy, and if it has set too much, it is really hard to work and you are left with the cold marks of the trowel.

I wet the brush again and start brushing horizontally across a section of the wall. The water starts to penetrate the wall and what I have started calling the 'liquid moment ' approaches. And then I am immersed in it as the render starts to move under my brushstrokes, small lumps are smoothing out, depressions being filled and tiny quartz stones buried under the liquid layer. Miles' spastic rhythmic solo reverberates through the empty house, through the pores in my skin, leaving goose bumps in its wake. My brushstrokes match the pulse of the music, I am the bassist's funky groove, I am the wailing trumpet solo, I am the drummer shuffling his brushes across the snare, I am the wall melting into the door and going fluidly around the corner... I am my house breathing...

The song ends as I am dipping the brush into the bucket of water and in the silence I look around, from the kitchen right through the 20 metres to the far lounge room wall. I see the insect shaped series of half hexes I have built stretching out in front of me, finally getting the last layer, the final skin. I see the soft rounded 45-degree corners melting into straight sections of wall; I see the walls falling into windows, melting together into a single organic thing. I see, for the first time, my imagination made real.

Herbie Hancock's *Chameleon* eases up out of the speakers like a limousine pulling out onto Park Avenue, I wipe the excess water off my brush and hit the wall with it and this time it is a straight ahead kind of pulse and the wall disappears beneath my brush once again...

For 7 weeks I have been rendering this house, every wall, two to three layers on each. For 7 weeks, 7 days a week, 10 hours a day, I had been mixing render and dancing with the walls. My injured arm ached continually but I had stopped noticing it as I delved deeper each day into the house addiction. I look at my arm and thank it for giving me a benchmark for what pain really is. *A sore arm after a day's work is a walk in the fucking park, man*, I mutter to myself, and watch the soft lines the brush leaves on the wall.

I see car headlights coming down the driveway through the pair of coloured glass windows either side of the front door. They turn from yellow to blue to red and blast my wall with colour. Goes well with Herbie, I think, as the car comes to a stop outside and I hear the familiar sound of our car doors slamming shut. Suddenly the door bursts open and

Hannah is running through it at a fast jog. I smile and wave to her and put my brush and bucket down. I can see Cass and Em heading over to the studio together, our very cramped home for the last year.

I look up at Han and she is dancing to Herbie, a wild flailing of her arms and she's laying down the funk with her legs. She dances over to me.

"Hello Daaaadddyyy!" still dancing.

"Hey sweetheart, how was your day?" as I mimic her moves.

"Awesome Dad, guess what?"

"Um let's see, you're learning the banjo now?"

She laughs hysterically. "No Dad, don't be silly!"

"OK, what happened?" as I walk over and turn *Chameleon* down a couple of notches.

"Well, first thing was that at school Carly told me I was not her friend anymore, then we were on the monkey bars hanging upside down by our legs and she tried to grab me to push me off and she fell off and everybody laughed and then I made a new friend called Christy, and then the bell went and we went back to the classroom and Mr Quill was playing the banjo again and I told him the joke you told me to tell him about 'what do you throw a drowning banjo player? A couple of fold-back speakers' and he laughed, Dad, and then he went all serious and back to being Mr Quill... Dad? I think Mr Quill is a lot like you, like you are cheeky boys and that!"

I look at her with theatrical disapproval. "What do you mean?"

I raise an eyebrow and she squeals with laughter and I make a move like I'm going to chase her.

She jumps up and says, "Oh and guess what, Dad? We went Christmas shopping today and we bought you a present! And I'm not allowed to tell you what it is..."

"Oh really?"

"Yes Dad, and it's not even a hammock!"

I run around the house chasing her and laughing, kicking over trays and buckets and tripping over drop cloths. She runs out the door screaming with laughter.

Let the liquid moments in, I mutter, just gotta let them in...

The Raffle
20 years ago

By the second week of isolation, I had started placing the TV on such an angle that, when it was off, I could see the reflection of people's legs as they walked by my room. I had started writing with my left hand, a messy concoction of lines like a madman's ransom note. There were 67 bricks outside my window. I would play back what I had recorded and stare out the window and wonder who the fuck was on the tape, because it didn't sound like me at all. And there were three of them, three different voices that puzzled me with their ramblings.

The nurses had slowly been reducing my morphine and replacing it with Mercindol, an ugly synthetic that made me angry and depressed and unable to focus my eyes at all. So they gave me Proladone instead, a powerful suppository that lasted 8 hours, double that of the morphine. After the first one I stopped letting the nurses insert them up my arse and did it myself. That way I could just slide them up the crack of my arse in front of the nurses so they could tick a box on my file and I could store the drugs up, saving them for when the walls started to moan and the pain was bad enough to stop me from writing or staring at the dead TV screen. If I used two at once I would be flying, even the bricks throbbed contentedly when I did this and the room would become a huge velvet cushion. I had started to settle in to my madness.

Eventually it came time to disconnect my arm from my stomach. Somehow or other what was left of the exposed flesh on my arm had stuck to the flesh of my stomach and the nurse had to separate them before the operation could happen. The foam they had put between the flesh was the problem it seemed, it being stuck by something called 'serus ooze' and I must say there is something beautiful about those two words together, even though it meant large pain coming my way. The first attempt to remove it by the nurse resulted in the most painful thing I had experienced, like I could feel the flesh tearing off me. The howl that accompanied it stopped the nurse in her tracks and off she scurried again, this time returning with the sister. She was a large woman with the most beautiful kind eyes set in a chubby, compassionate face. She had been very good to me, had always got the morphine for me when I asked and had actually sat one time and asked me how I was coping.

This time she has a large syringe on a tray in one hand and the other hand on her hip as she stands in the doorway.

"Well good afternoon, Tony, I hear you're giving Melinda here a hard time?" looking at the nurse who had regained a little composure and was looking self assured in the presence of her boss.

"Hey sister," I smile at her, "You're gonna have to knock me out for this one and you're the only one here who could do it with one punch!" I bare my cheek to her playfully, giving her a wink.

She walks over to the bed, takes the syringe in her hand and says, "I've got a better idea." as she plunges the needle into my arm.

Next thing I know I am plummeting down a tunnel and the deeper I go the darker it gets. I can see the light from the top fade into the distance and I am falling, falling very fucking fast. The rocks I pass are a blur of cold reality, the screeching I can hear below me getting louder and louder. I can hear my breathing, slow and constant, like I am asleep. But I am far from it.

The darkness turns a dirty green as it gets lighter and I brace myself... Then I have landed and I can't remember landing. I am just here all of a sudden. I look around me. I seem to be in some sort of jungle, massive trees form a canopy above me and thick undergrowth is everywhere in front of me... I can hear the sounds of frightened animals running through the jungle, all of it coming from the same direction. The screeching of birds and other animals fills my head with fear and anguish, and it is then that I notice the change. I look down at my nose, it has fur covering it and whiskers growing out the sides. In bewilderment I look down and notice I am crouching on all fours, my arms no longer there, transformed into legs covered in fur with large claws sticking out the ends of them... And I am scared.

Suddenly I am shaking, my whole body is shaking, no, the whole ground is shaking. Large shadows are moving towards me very fast, and I take flight, running expertly on all four legs, darting between bushes and shrubs, my whole body straining as I go as fast as I can. The shadows loom over the ground in front of me, getting closer and closer. Inexplicably, I slide to a stop, turn around to see what's coming at me. I can't believe what I am seeing... huge dinosaurs are crashing through the primeval jungle, banging into each other in their terror, careering forward like dodgem cars at an amusement park. I turn and run for my life...

When I come to the nurse and sister have stepped back, their mouths agape, the sister holding the blood-covered foam with a set of tweezers.

Groggily I say, "What the fuck? Where did I just go?"

My heart is racing as I look down and see a new piece of foam separating my arm and stomach.

"Holy shit!" the nurse chips in, "You should've heard the sounds coming out of your mouth! You were chanting something in some other language, then you were screeching like a bird, then you were singing a strange song... Boy, you sure are nuts!" and then she laughs, a 'can't believe it' laugh and turns to the sister, who looks knowingly at me with a raised eyebrow and says "Well, I guess we won't wait two weeks to change the foam next time!"

After they have gone I stare out the window at the 37th brick, as if the answer could be found there. *What the fuck is happening to me? I felt so comfortable in that fur, it seemed natural to me. I had been there before that's for sure. But when? I have no memory of this, nor could it be found in my dreams, what the fuck is happening...?*

I drift off to sleep to the sound of rubber-soled shoes on polished linoleum.

A Desert and a Slide Guitar
4 years ago

Bazza's got a huge Maori sitting next to him on the bench seat and the lights have changed to daylight hues as he yells to the Maori, "Can you hurry up and close the door mate. Look!" pointing to the imaginary rear view mirror.

The Maori looks back as he shuts the door and says "What?" just as a huge projected image of a desert road train appears and barrels towards them, a massive plume of red dust in its wake and spilling out to the sides making it appear like a giant frill necked lizard bearing down on them.

"Shit!" the Maori exclaims. "What do we do, bro?"

The low rumble of the truck builds until you can barely hear Bazza saying, "Wind up the window and hold tight, my new friend!"

Lights flash, then go dim. The truck sound bellows out of the speakers with such force that even I am starting to flinch in anticipation as the projected truck heads straight towards the camera, until all you can see is the front bull bar and grill of the truck with the 'Mack' dog emblem in mid-pounce dead centre. The sound dies off towards the back of the theatre, the lights go back up to full and this time it's a reddish-brown light that bathes Bazza and his new hitchhiker.

"Farken' hell bro, that was intense. I think that was the prick who didn't stop and pick me up a day back... rude cunt, there I was in the middle of nowhere and nothing, no car or truck in sight for hours and then this prick goes past and next thing I know I'm covered in shit, bro!"

Bazza replies with, "Umm, don't mean to be rude but HAVE YOU SEEN THE SIZE OF THOSE THINGS? Eight, sometimes ten trailers on and doing 140km/hr. Takes 5k's to slow 'em down and fuckin' ages to get 'em back up to speed. I wouldn't stop for anyone or anything either!" He continues as he takes a finger off the wheel and points at the audience in front of him. "Look at the roo carcasses all over the place, it's not the grey nomads killing 'em with their shiny caravans and white socks and sandals, it's those fuckin' monsters! So, what's your name anyway?"

He looks across at his Maori passenger. He is huge, maybe 6'4", muscular but a touch pudgy and covered in tattoos, which are all over his face and neck, Bazza notices that there are even little tattoos on each knuckle of his hand.

"Me name's Warren, but you can call me 'Wazza'."

Bazza laughs, "Bazza and Wazza on a road to nowhere! "

After a moment Wazza asks, "So where ya goin', bro?"

"To my salvation, Wazza, the back door exit, I'm putting my cue in the rack, mate... cancer's gone right through me... If I sit it out I may have a month. But fuck that! I'm not gonna end up a morphine skeleton, fuck that for a joke!"

Wazza looks as if he is sorry he asked, then brightens up and says, "Well, I'm gonna to work on a prawn boat. It'll be sweet: plenty of dosh and then the chicks'll be all over me, mate, it'll be sweet."

Bazza looks at him wryly and says, "So, how long you been outa jail?"

Wazza looks at him, dumbfounded, turns and looks out the 'window' at the audience and looks slightly dejected.

The time passes in silence, day turns to night, Bazza goes through the various states of driving... alert, sleepy, fearful, angry, forgetful. At times he claws the wheel, at others he lets it slide through his finger-tips, he eyes go wide in fear, then go dull with sickness and tiredness, until he looks 90. The lights throw deep canyons just below his eyes making his face look disembodied, floating through the cool desert night.

I'm above the stage again in the flys, right at the front of stage. I have crawled across the steel girders and perched myself dead centre of the stage. From here I can see the thoughts escaping Harry's head before he can get to them, the sweat pouring down his back. Wazza's is bone dry, seemingly unaffected by the 120 stage lights pouring their beams onto him. Bazza starts fidgeting behind the wheel, gripping it hard, scratching his head and making the long wisps of grey hair dance out into the light they are bathed in.

"You see mate, I've been ripped off. Worked my whole fuckin' life with just enough money to get by. I rent a small place in Gawler and I've lived there for 30 fuckin' years and I haven't even grown a fuckin' pot plant in that time, never... Never lived a life, Wazza, I got stuck in 'just getting by' thinkin' that when I retire I'll be on the gravy train and then I'll have the life that everyone else seems to have... I thought, like everyone else, that my 20's would last forever, that my luck pulling the ladies will keep on forever, that my dick always get hard when I wanted it to, that my looks would hold and just improve… couldn't have been more wrong if I tried. I mean, for fuck's sake, look at me, riddled with cancer, half the man I used to be and I didn't even make it to retirement age…"

His head droops down and rests on the wheel.

"Aah c'mon bro, it's not that bad, think of the good shit, man, that's the stuff that kept me goin' in jail. It's how you look at what happens to you and what you do with it, you should know this shit, you're and old cunt and that!"

Bazza looks at his passenger warily, then says, "Oh fuck, I've picked up a friggin' philosopher, a tattooed ex-con philosopher! Gonna call you Socrates from now on!"

"Who?" Wazza asks.

"Never mind. Just watch out for yourself, make sure you don't go numb, Wazza, and forget to live a life…"

"Got it covered bro, got it covered."

All this time the lights of oncoming traffic have been sporadically bathing our characters in a glaring off-white colour. As Bazza says, "…don't go numb", the colour changes to congo blue and hits them from behind, then fades slowly to black.

***

Later, at home, the smooth, self-assured Hammond organ intro of Tom Waits' 'Frank's Wild Years' fills my lounge room with its pulsating cheesiness. I sit alone smoking in the dark, the only light coming from the glow of the dying fire as Tom's lyrics kick in.

Frank settled down in the valley
He hung his wild years on a nail that he drove
through his wife's forehead
Sold used office furniture out there on San
Fernando road
Assumed a 30,000 dollar loan at 15 and a
quarter per-cent
Put a down payment on a little two bedroom
place...

I am smiling now as Tom lays it down. It is 2 a.m but it feels like early evening despite the weariness in my bones and the dull pounding in my head. I picture the outer suburbs of Los Angeles.

His wife was a spent piece of used jet trash
Made good Bloody Marys, kept her mouth shut
most of the time
Had a little Chihuahua named Carlos that had
some kind of skin disease and was totally blind
Had a thoroughly modern kitchen, self cleaning
oven the whole bit
Frank drove a little sedan, they were so happy...

The cheesy Hammond has this little showbiz style kick at the end of each phrase.

It's the small things, always the small things, I think ,as I grin through smoke.

One night Frank was on his way home from
work
Stopped at the liquor store, picked up a couple
of Mickey's Big Mouths
Drank 'em in the car on the way to the Shell
station, got a gallon gas in a can

79

*Drove home, doused everything in the house,
torched it
Parked across the street laughing, watching it
burn
All Halloween orange and chimney red
Frank put on a top-40 station
Got on the Hollywood freeway and headed
north
Never could stand that dog…*

Afterwards, I walk to the kitchen in the dark, toss the empty can into the recycle bin. No need to creep, there's no one else here, no one for 2 kilometres, yet I walk silently and expertly through my dark, empty house to the bathroom where I look into the mirror, see my tired, worn face; my road-face. Fuck, I look like those guys hopping out of the truck a few days ago, except add 20 years.

Tone, I say to myself, *you've got to get the fuck out of here, man.*

A Beach in Thailand
Present

A bird has landed on the log and is balancing itself when another one lands. The log doesn't change its gentle rolling movement at all, instead the birds walk up and down its gnarly trunk with the ocean swells, shaking water off their feathers as they go.

How long have I been here? I think, even though a knowing smile runs swiftly across my face as I think it, the realisation that there is no time that matters anymore, only this time right now. I could've been here for hours or minutes and every time I see myself lost in thought I wonder if I will ever get back again, and then that doesn't matter either.

I blow my nose football style and wipe the excess off on my arm, the good arm, and try to clear my throat of the gunk from crying. I dry my eyes and watch the birds cleaning themselves. One of them has its mouth open wide and is flapping its wings from time to time. But there is no squawking, no sound at all. Then I notice the other bird has something wrapped around its leg and is trying to pull it off with its beak. Finally after quite a lot of pulling, tugging and hopping around, what looks like a piece of blue plastic gets flung into the water next to them... Soon enough, the bird is plunging its beak into the open mouth of the other bird and this time what looks like a plastic bottle cap is flung into the water, followed by a squeal of relief.

I look at the debris-strewn beach around me and wonder how many thousands of other beaches are like this ocean, this South East Asian soup we all eat out of, that my beautiful log has found itself lost in.

Lost in an ocean of rubbish…

The Release
3 years ago

Michelle's bony legs are wrapped tightly around my waist, her arms are resting on my shoulders and she is laughing at my antics. The street is full of all sorts of people on their way out to restaurants, bars, clubs, shows and I am greeting them as we walk, each new person getting a different accent, sometimes a whole different character if the urge takes me there. And tonight I am on the edge of something; it almost feels like I am tripping.

The next one along is a guy in a business suit and I can see the glazed eyes and his half drunk lag of a walk from 5 steps away. I clear my throat and my voice drops an octave. I clear my throat again, this time theatrically.

"Oh I say old chap, do you have a moment?" in my best British radio announcer voice.

The man stops in his tracks.

"Oh thank you ever so much. Terribly kind of you. Now," I pronounce, "my friend and I have a small problem. As you can see my lovely companion has decided that I piggy-back her up this street, this lovely little street. Who could've thought this could exist in such a god-forsaken country? Anyway, my friend here wants me to find a club, let's say, that is rather unusual. You see, old man, she wants me to suspend her from a ceiling naked and spin her around and whip her hard as she passes and she wants me to wear a ballerina's dress and when I saw you I thought to myself, this man can help us..."

Whilst I am saying this I am looking the man up and down appreciatively.

He looks at us mouth agape and stumbles on past us as Michelle snickers loudly and smacks me on the arse, almost like a 'giddy up' smack, and then says, "I think my eyebrow got a hard-on, it's permanently raised!"

The next passer-by gets 'innocent down to earth bloke from Swan Hill'.

"Yeah, s'cuse me love?"

A woman with short hair and wearing a man's suit and groovy glasses stops.

"How ya goin'? D'ya know where I can take me girlfriend for a feed round 'ere? Y'know, bit of a fancy joint with waiters and shit?"

She falls for it and smiles condescendingly at me, saying,

"Um, what do you like to eat? There's a good..."

"I fuckin' love me meat," winking at her, "and so does Shazza, don't ya love?" looking up at Michelle.

"I fuckin' love YOUR meat, Shane," she drawls, licking her lips.

The woman walks off disgustedly as Michelle kicks her legs out playfully, like a child at an amusement park.

"Damnit, I had a whole monologue ready!" I say, in exasperation.

And then the next one. An emo girl wearing $1000 worth of clothes, looking sullen.

"Everything's fucked," I say to her dejectedly, "Think I'll go write some poetry then jump in front of the 9.30 train to Springvale. My girl here's gonna film my body being smashed apart by the train, just thought you should know..."

We skip off from her, whistling the whistle from Kill Bill.

Soon enough we are standing outside the restaurant-bar that my sister works at, and I am getting my phone out and looking for her number as I say to Michelle, "Fancy a cocktail or two?" I put her down on her wobbly legs at the same time.

"Hi bro!" my sister voice pipes into my ear, "This is a nice surprise, how are you?"

"Mand, I'm fuckin' awesome and I've got another surprise for you. I'm standing outside your restaurant right now!"

***

My sister looks good, even happy, as she walks down the front steps towards us, holding out her arms. As she hugs me she says,

"So, how did it go?"

I whisper "Not now, Mand, not now." I pull back and look at her.

"You look great Mand." Turning to Michelle, who is looking a little confused, I say, "This is my friend Michelle, from Dance North."

My sister holds out her hand to Michelle and says, "Oh wow, I just saw 'Nightcafe' last month, great work!"

Michelle is caught by surprise and smiles, looks at my sister for a moment and says, "Thanks. Thanks a lot."

"And this is my sister, Amanda."

Michelle looks relieved as I carry her down the stairs into this funky little bar decorated with artistic swirls of material hanging off the ceiling and walls. The light is about as low as you can get without it being called dark. I put Michelle down at a table and go order the first round of drinks, saying to the barman, "Do you do tabs here, might be easier?"

"No worries sir..."

Several drinks and a hundred raves later and I am feeling buoyant, elated and very drunk. I see a green pair of 1950's shoes coming down the stairs and legs, long legs, disappearing into the ruffled edges of a vintage dress. There is something familiar about the walk and my eyes light up when I see that it is an old friend of mine whom I haven't seen in years. A French woman called Catherine that used to live nearby. I call her over. I had forgotten about her olive shaped green eyes. I had forgotten about the mischievous, cheeky Catherine.

After greetings and intros, she sits and as I order another round of drinks I say, "This is gonna be a great night. I mean, fuck, it already is!"

***

It is now 3a.m, the streets are nearly empty as we stumble down the front steps of the bar laughing. I am teetering the most with Michelle on my back, who is doing her best to wrestle me from behind as we go down. As we walk towards Michelle's hotel I can hear the sound of Catherine's heels echoing in front of us, every three or four clicks she drags the heel before laying it down again and I start to shuffle to the rhythm, she sees me and gives it more flow, Michelle steering me from side to side. Every now and then Catherine comes close and bumps us playfully with her hips, those fluid French hips swinging around the empty laneway in front of us.

Strangely I am not tired even though I have been up for 24 hours. There is a fire burning inside of me, an almost fierce desperation to stay in this moment, and ride it out. We dance all the way to the hotel, even dancing as the lift takes us to the 25th floor.

I sit down on the couch and gently lean back as Michelle releases herself from the piggy-back posture and slumps drunkenly back against the cushions. Catherine is fishing through the fridge and throwing out the contents onto the floor until we hear "Aah, viola!" and she is back in the room holding up three cold glasses and saying, "Nightcap anyone?"

She kneels up on the couch next to us holding two of the glasses out to us, grinning mischievously as she pulls a flask out of her handbag and then flings the bag across the room. She lets out a giggle.

"Mescal, anyone?"

We go in close for the 'cheers'. All looking at each other, we down our shots. Michelle wraps her arms around me again and says, "Thanks for a brilliant night."

"It's me who should be thanking the two of you," I slur whilst licking the inside of my shot glass, searching for more. "And I don't ever want this to end!"

We talk feverishly about the stuff that inspires us as the flask is emptied. We race through great films and books, pause in front of great paintings and weep as Michelle describes the feeling of performing your own work on a stage in front of a thousand people. Catherine regales us with tales of street art in Paris and the wild experimental music scene to be found down small laneways, in out-of-the-way places. I talk about getting lost in liquid moments, that they could be found everywhere, in everything. And that I was sharing one now, with two beautiful women on the 25th floor, a million cocktails drunk, a thousand stories told, a hundred ways to strangle life and hold its red/ blue face up to your own and shriek in delight, knowing it was all possible, anything was possible.

Michelle is drifting off, curled up in the foetal position as Catherine talks about her first love, the first time her heart leapt up and out of her body, infecting her and those around her. I watch her lips move as she talks and for a moment I relish the thought of what could be.

As we watch the first sun throw long streaks of orange light across the old buildings below us, I mutter, "I am waking up…"

"Yes, my friend, you are…"

Sledgehammer
40 years ago

As we get closer to the white car I see the insect screen my father put over the windscreen before we went on holiday just a few short months ago. For an instant, I see myself on the balcony of a hotel on my hands and knees, playing with my milk truck. I loved that truck. It had doors that opened on the side and little bottles of milk that even made the clinking sound when you pushed it fast, and I am flinging the truck repeatedly into the balustrade. Every time I go to pick it up, I notice the milkman driving the truck is STILL smiling. I hear my father yelling at me to stop, which of course just eggs me on. I grit my teeth and fling the truck with all the available strength in my 4-year-old body. Next thing I know it is going over the edge of the balcony. I race to the edge to watch it, it seems to take forever, 'cause before it even hits the floor my father has run across to stop me going over, he is pulling my legs and I am holding the edge with my hands and chin, resisting. A strange calm overtakes me as I see my milk truck hit the ground and disintegrate. He pulls me back, stands me up and smacks me three times, so hard my whole body is pushed forward with each whack. "That'll serve you right, you little shit. See what happens when you smash things?"

I look through the dirty insect screen at the woman sitting inside our car. She is filing her nails and looking wary as we approach her, Nadia's stagger has turned to a trot once we hit the road surface. My stare fixes on this woman and she stares back at me with a 'what's your problem?' look. This must be the woman who stole my Dad... My gaze shifts across to the driver's side- mirror, I line it up and slide down off Nadia's hip a touch. We are no more than 5 steps away now and I pull my right leg back kick the mirror. I don't feel the blow at all... I hear the mirror hit the ground and slide, I look back over my shoulder and now the woman has a 'what the fuck?' look and she's screaming at me but all I can hear now is the shuffling of Nadia's sandals as she continues across the street, seemingly oblivious to the sliding mirror going past...

I am staring up at the streetlights that ring the Court, they have a circle of haze around them and a thousand insects courting their death. My senses are tingling, everything is in slow motion, like I have climbed inside the moment. I am watching and I am in it at the same time. The mirror comes to a stop in the gutter in front of the gaping-mouthed Sampson's. I hear the exhausted scream of my mother pleading, 'No!' as another almighty smash reverberates down the dark suburban street.

Liquid Moments
14 years ago

"Daddy, can we put our music on instead of the weird stuff you listen to?"

"By all means... what you got in mind, sweetheart?"

"Um, I think Hanson, Dad. Zac is sooooo cute!" Han runs off and I can hear her bounding down the stairs and running across to the little studio we had been living in for the last two years. I wince at the thought of the next hour, or possibly more if she hits repeat, listening to the latest pop sensation.

Shit, I think, millionaires before they hit 15 years old, probably be all jaded with substance abuse issues by 19 and writing the first autobiography at 21.

I watch Cass laying the drop sheets on her bedroom floor in preparation to paint her walls. She had chosen her colour (light blue) and helped as I added the watered down PVA glue, natural off-white clay and natural oxide powder together and mixed them in a bucket with a long mixing attachment on the end of a drill.

"How come we are making our own paint, Daddy, instead of buying it in the shop like everyone else?"

She wipes the paint spots off her face and hands as the mixer does its job and I slowly add the blue until she thinks it is 'blue' enough.

"Well, Cass, I can make 20 litres of paint for 10 dollars and it's natural, no chemicals, you could probably drink the stuff, not that I'm saying you should! 20 litres of bought paint is closer to 200 dollars, by the way! Besides, it looks so much better."

"Gee Dad, what are you going to do with the money you save, buy me and Hannah new bikes maybe?"

Straight faced I say, "Too late, I'm afraid. I'm saving it for a time machine!"

"Oh Dad!" She rolls her eyes at me and laughs.

Cass lays out the drop sheets neatly and gets a little bit cross if it has a bulge anywhere. She is wearing an old shirt of mine, and a bandana to cover her hair. Finally she is satisfied, and she looks up at me, and smiles.

"I'm ready, Dad, can I start?"

Just then Hanson comes blasting out of the speakers and I can hear Hannah bounding back up the stairs.

I shout over the music, "Go for it!"

Hannah's room is the opposite. Dropsheets haphazardly thrown around, her bandana is slipping down the back of her head, and fine blond wisps of hair are sticking out as she and I dip our brushes into her bucket of purple paint, Han swaying to the infectious beat of '*Mmmm-bop*'.

After a while, she asks me, "Dad, how come I don't have any grandfathers?"

She slaps the thick purple paint on the vast dividing wall between her and Cass's bedrooms. I am cutting in around the doorframe, once again reflecting on the pure-white directness of our second born child when I say,

"As you know, your Mum's papa Bricky died before you were born…"

"Yeah I know Dad, but what about YOUR dad?"

"Mine ran away…"

"What from, what did he run away from, Dad?"

"Maybe he was running away from himself, maybe he didn't know who he was anymore, maybe he didn't want to have a family, a mortgage, a job, maybe he was just a negligent prick who didn't care about anything except himself. I'm not really sure Han, I haven't seen him since I was 4, when he smashed the house up…"

"Did it make you angry, Dad? "

I thought for a while, then said, "Yes Han it did, but I didn't let it get me down. I rose up instead…"

"What's 'rose up' Daddy?"

"When you don't let something beat you, instead you use it to make you strong. I feel sorry for him now," as I feel a tear welling up, "because he didn't get to meet you and Cass…"

"Yeah Dad, I feel sorry for him too. Is he alive?"

"Not sure. Uncle Craigy heard that he was living in a caravan park on his own, drinking a slab of beer a day and a bottle of port and talking on a CB radio. Sounds like it all worked out for him, huh?"

"Boy that's really sad, Daddy, why did he throw his family away? I could've had a grandpa…"

"But you have, you've got the most interesting 'grandpa' of all your friends, you've got Jacko!"

I thought of my Canadian/ American Indian ex-boxer jazz guitarist friend who had been dropping in every Sunday, sitting on the veranda with me and my girls and playing old jazz tunes on his Macaferri guitar. His favourite was "*Sunny Side of the Street*" and he sang just like Satchmo. He would have a smile from ear to ear as he sang.

"Oh yeah!" Han screams over the music and she mimics his singing and plays air guitar with her paintbrush, "On the sunny side of the street..."

Her antics have me laughing.

"I guess Han, you find the family you don't have in others, and they are often better than the real thing!"

I fill my brush with paint as the Hanson CD starts again, racing up the stairs and filling the bedrooms with the marketed sound of childhood innocence.

"Yeah I think we are lucky Dad, don't you think?"

"More than you know, sweetheart, more than you know..."

The Raffle
20 years ago

It seems that half the ward is now in isolation as they wheel me up the corridor. All the nurses now have on the mask, gloves and gown combination.

Was I dreaming? Had I infected everyone?

Pete is still here. He sits upright when he sees me coming, I hold out my good hand and he takes it.

Ever shake a fingerless hand? It's jarring, I can tell you, very jarring. That lone leg is still resting up in the corner. He pulls a flask from under his pillow, passes it over. I take a belt.

"Thanks mate, hey, you know what we should do with that leg there?" I pass the flask back.

"What mate, sell it? Who'd buy a fifteen year old artificial leg?" He takes a long pull on the flask, gags, and coughs heavily.

"I think we should raffle it!"

Later that night we find a groggy throat cancer victim to help us out. A few promptings from the flask and he takes the leg across and places it roughly in the Christmas tree. Under the night-lights it looks very beautiful sticking out of that tree. You can just see the red 'Christmas raffle' scrawled across its thigh. It makes it look like the tree is just waiting for the other leg to sprout, and it'll be gone.

***

The pain has mostly gone, but I have made sure the morphine hasn't. Pete is still waiting for his trip upstairs. The sun is losing its battle with the haze as Melbourne's summer sets in. The leg juts crudely out of the sagging tree. People see it there and look disturbed. Pete and I snicker to ourselves, and he tells me stories of his drinking bouts in his 17th floor Commission flat. I watch the gleam in his eyes and wait for my next morphine shot.

"You see, the lifts hardly ever worked in my building, mate. They were stuffed. Gordon, me next door neighbour, used to get the wine for me and we'd sit around and drink it. He was me best mate, Tone... He was me only mate. We got along real well. He'd been drinking for years, ever since his wife and child got squashed by a truck one day. I knew he was sick, but shit, I wasn't real well meself. He used to help me wash and feed me dog. He was like a brother, but better. He got me my first fuck, got a nurse drugged up on horse pills and she fucked everyone in sight. Yeah a good mate..."

He stared at a spot on the floor.

"Ended up moving in with me. That way we had more to spend at the bottle shop. He used to call me his 'little mate'. In the mornings we'd go out on the balcony and watch the sun come up, pissed as farts, and vomit over the railing. All out Asian neighbours would be out on their balconies doing Tai Chi, or whatever it is..."

"Fuck!" I laughed.

It was a vivid image. A pretty nurse came in so I put on my 'I need something for the pain' performance whilst sneaking glances at the light streaming through her uniform. As she left to get the shot, I realise I had forgotten what it was like to have a hard-on.

A Desert and a Slide Guitar
4 years ago

Harry appears out of the dirty blue backstage light and walks towards the props area with an almost feverish intensity and a hungry look on his face. He then looks slightly bewildered as he searches the table for something, mutters to himself, then wanders off towards the set area as if summoned by an invisible benevolence that only he can hear... I watch him intensely as he effortlessly negotiates the dark backstage recesses as if he has lived here all his life. This is Harry's world, his element. If there is a dreaming place for us all then I was standing in the middle of Harry's. I watch the Bek, the Stage Manager, carrying herbal teas to the dressing rooms where needy actresses awaited the placation the SM she served up with every chamomile infusion.

"Room temperature sushi..." I mutter to myself, my phrase for the absolutely fucking ridiculous requests of the 'artistes' at times. The ones on the edge of fame and fortune seemed to have the more insane requests, delivered with a veritable truckload of attitude. I remember one international children's show where the technical rider list was 2 pages long and the dressing rooms/ actors requirements 17 pages long, including suggested menus, types of incense, organic wheatgrass shakes, a yoga instructor, suggested temperatures and even suggested colour schemes for the rooms, for fuck's sake... The more famous they were, the less affected they seemed to be, there was an almost humble acceptance of any variation of the grand rider requests they started with.

One comedian I worked with who came through the venue for years started by asking for a stock standard microphone on a stand and a follow spotlight. As his fame rose and he was filling auditoriums twice a night, his rider became increasingly complicated and ridiculous: sets were added, projection, two or three expensive microphones, lighting cues, set moves, and backstage crew... and he was still telling the same jokes. At one stage he was touring with his pet monkey, which would be let loose in the dressing rooms whilst he snorted coke and blew ganja smoke in the monkey's face. And with the coke racing through his brain, the arrogant, rude and obnoxious behaviour increased to the point where on one occasion I had to physically restrain Johnno, the lighting tech, from launching himself at him.

One of his 'gags' was about different types of stairs. There were 'showbiz' stairs and just ordinary stairs. We rehearsed not once or twice, but 10 times through the sound and lighting cues so that when he walked to the 'showbiz' stairs centre stage (a set of treads going nowhere) and he stepped on the first step, a spotlight would go on and Sinatra's "*New York New York*" would come over the speakers. Then he would walk over to the stairs that led from the stage to the auditorium and 'hilariously' no music or showbiz lighting would go on.

After the second rehearsal we had nailed it but he insisted on doing it over and over, telling us that 'most techs were a bunch of fucking idiots but we weren't... yet...'

Even I felt like dropping him.

When it came to the 'gag' we did our job perfectly, the gag got a good laugh and then he told the audience they wouldn't believe how long it took the techs to get it right that afternoon. As I heard him saying this I said to Johnno: "You should never harm the messenger... OK, Johnno, during the encore when he does the gag again, lets reverse it on him..."

Johnno snickered and said, "No worries, let's do it!"

And so we did. At first the comedian thought that we had fucked up, looked to the audience as if to say, 'See, your techs are shit', and then it hits him and looking straight up at the bio–box he strides across his stage to the ordinary stairs, whereupon the music and lights go on, and this time I pump the sound and Johnno flashes the spotlight. We get a bigger laugh than he did. He gets on the mic and points to us up in the bio-box, screaming, "I'll see you pricks after the show!"

Johnno and I are rolling on the floor laughing.

Within a year he was back to just the mic, stand and spotlight.

***

"Pssst Tone, over here!"

I peer into the darkness and eventually I see Harry, sitting down under the huge Styrofoam tree we carted out of the truck days ago, his legs pulled up under his chin, his arms clasped around them.

"Sit down, mate," patting a spot under the tree next to him. "You ever heard about this tree Tone?"

"Nope, 'fraid not."

"Well," Harry says dramatically, "There's this mad bloke out in the desert who hates feral cats.

Fuckin' despises them, so much so, he has devoted his life to killing as many of them as he can. Hangs 'em upside down in a dead tree in the middle of fuckin' nowhere..."

I look up at the 'tree' above our heads and it is then that I see the cat shaped paper lanterns hanging off the dead branches like demented flowers.

"Lets the eagles and hawks and crows pull them to shreds whilst he drinks whisky and cleans his shotgun, whistling an old show tune from the '50's. He's this gnarly nugget of a bloke who has lived rough in the bush his whole life and he loves Doris Day! Fucking hilarious... and he is one of the happiest blokes I've ever met and I reckon I know why, Tone. He wakes up every morning, and he not only knows who he is and what he wants to do, but he fuckin' loves it as well. A real gem, that one."

"Fuck Harry, I'm 40 and I still don't know what I want to do."

"And let's hope you never do, Tone, let's hope you never do!" He grins at me through the darkness.

"Harry, do you ever feel like you're not really there, like all this 'stuff' is happening around you and it's like you're numb or frozen or something?"

"Mate, I'm an actor, I thrive in a world of make–believe, fuck I don't think I can even distinguish anymore... if I wasn't doing what I am doing I probably would've been locked up years ago, jammed full of tranquillisers and drooling out the side of my mouth! An actor has to get inside and outside the character at the same time, thoroughly immersed, but also watching the immersion like a spectator..."

"So what are you running away from Harry?"
He thinks for a while and then replies.

"The fear of not living a life mate, the fear of a homogenised non-existence, the fear of going through the motions, the fear of forgetting what a twisted bizarre miracle life is…"

I stare at Harry through the darkness, grin at him and say,

"Harry, I'm glad I met you."

A Beach in Thailand
Present

I pull my gaze away from the log and look along the beach. All around me now the debris is piling up as the swollen waves spread it relentlessly onto the sand. I realise I am sitting like Harry was under the feral cat tree those few short years ago. Was it 3 or 10 years ago, was it last week? How long have I been here? A smirk crosses my face when I realise that it doesn't matter anymore, everything is now, there is nothing else...

I can see my friends way off in the distance, small moving coloured blobs not much bigger than the piles surrounding them. My grin widens as I imagine all the treasures they have found. I look at the small pile of driftwood next to me. I marvel at the amazing vibrant colours painted one on top of the other, the ocean and the sun randomly peeling away the layers so that some were red, blue and purple, some green, yellow and orange... I imagine the force of an ocean that can hit a fishing boat and rip sections of it off like these, toss them around for years in the currents and then relinquish them onto the beach in monsoon season... And yet it doesn't have the power to hurl my log onto its final resting place...

Off in the distance I see Phee Noi wrestling a large piece of wood away from the vicious suck of the retreating waves. I see him raise an arm for help and then Phee Nan is helping him to roll the huge beast of a thing up onto the dry sand. There are lines of previous tides running up and down the beach, thin lines of debris delineating each one. I let my eyes follow one of them right back to where I am sitting, the line is dotted with hundreds of cigarette lighters which jump out at me due to their various translucent hues, the sun glancing off them, making them appear to be flashing. My heart is thumping, my ears ultra sensitive, the grin that must make me look insane preventing my lip from quivering. A massive wave of emotion wells up again inside of me, I look around for something, for help, for a shoulder, but there is none: just me, this log, and this beach. And my log continues to resist the pull of the current.

The Release
3 years ago

The rumble of the Duke echoes through the trees and across the paddocks as I cruise down the dirt road to home. It is late afternoon and the sun is creeping almost apologetically over the horizon, sending bands of light across the land. There hasn't been a show through the theatre in over a week and I am getting twitchy. I have been doing 9-5 and I've never been good with that. Something about the sameness of it, the peak hour traffic, the supermarket queues that seem to kill my spirit, push it to some limit of tolerance, and then I would be numb... Doing shows staved off the numbness. After 20 years, it had become a part of me to be working on shows with many others, the buzz of a short time frame to build the set, light it, top and tail it (rehearse just the beginning and end of each scene). Whatever it was, we did it. Arts workers are all misfits, we love working at night when everyone else is out being entertained. We work hard and party even harder, often all in the same day. It was not unusual to be having a beer at 3a.m on the loading dock after a 16 hour day, sharing a joint with the crew that were here for a day or two at most, telling gig stories and looking at the relentless white lines rushing across the surface of their eyeballs as they talked...

I used to be one of them, a touring tech, complete with road-face and road-sock, the latter of which had the pleasant effect of getting me a motel room to myself. Every day a new venue, a new sound system to work out how to use, new people, new town. You learn to hit the ground running and it does something to you. A lot of them didn't even have a base anymore, all their stuff was in storage, the girlfriend, having got fed up with them hardly ever being around, had left, and now home was the dark recesses of backstage, bathed in blue light and the glow from the laptops. Or an empty motel room. So addicted to the show, the rest of their lives falling away like autumn leaves. Now the shows came to me…

***

I am on my second bourbon by the time the sun has slinked away, turning the valley a deep, brooding mauve. I look out from the veranda at my garden, all overgrown and neglected. I see the 4 foot high grass and the broken ride on mower just sitting in the middle of it, the only cut grass being the trail the mower had left on what turned out to be its last journey. I look at the piles of rubbish and discarded building materials I had left 'randomly' scattered around to make the place look like shit. It was working… inside was just as bad, I had let the cobwebs take over the roof, chairs and tables. I had left piles of papers and dirty cups, overflowing ashtrays on the kitchen table, which is the first thing you see when you walk in.

This is what her valuer will see in the morning, I think, as I empty my bourbon can and head towards the fridge in search of another. There is the smell of a dead mouse to top it all off, the mouse having died some time ago behind the fridge and, well, I just hadn't gotten around to picking it up. It was funny because I couldn't even really smell it anymore, so accustomed had I become to it.

I walk back outside and plop myself drunkenly on the cobweb laden chair and wonder about the red back spiders that live inches from my butt under the chair. I look around at my creation, the piles of rubbish, the weeds, the drooping remnants of the sunflowers she had grown, piles of rocks next to half built garden walls, the upturned wheelbarrow in the long grass and it was then that it hits me. I have built a set, a look. I have designed all of this to make one person uncomfortable and tomorrow it's Showtime. I laugh to myself, sip some bourbon and peer out at the ride -on mower. Something not quite right about it, something not quite theatrical enough.

It was nearly dark before I have collected enough pieces to get started. For years I had been collecting these gnarly branches of trees that a disease had mutated and then strangled to death, leaving them hanging in the trees until they eventually fell to the ground, whereupon a scrounger such as myself would pick them up and marvel at the twisted beauty of each piece. Where the branch connected to the trunk would be transformed into a gnarly flower shaped thing, like a demented gothic hand. The locals called it 'mistletoe'.

I turned on the outside speakers, switched on the outside light so that I could see, and got to work.

I would look at each piece as if I were seeing it for the first time, then find a place on the mower to wedge it into. Before too long a lizard like shape started to form. The Nepalese world music pumping out of the speakers was inspiring me to the point where it seemed as if each piece was choosing me. The Spanish style guitars, congas, djembes, flutes and violins combined effortlessly into this global sound, part Spanish, part African, part blues, part reggae. It was a miraculous combination.

After a few hours I found myself brush cutting the grass around this huge frill necked lizard with a ride-on mower in its belly. It is around 11pm; I am drunk and watching as the cut grass reveals the thing more and more with each pass of the brush cutter. Finally I cut the motor and look at it. The demented hand shapes has been fanned out to form the frill-neck, four large mutated branches have sprung out to form legs and the rest bunched together to form the body.

It looks like it is ready to pounce on its prey, and tomorrow I am hoping it will.

The Raffle
20 years ago

I am driving fast along a dirt road. Warm gusts of air come in through the open windows. Lou Reed is coming through the speakers telling me I need " a busload of faith to get by"... cut to an image of a child playing with a toy car, pushing it back and forth across the carpeted floor and she is making 'vroom vroom' sounds as she hurls it forward... I round the final bend to home and in front of me I see a double bed in the middle of the road, a woman with a child nestled in the eternal moment of motherhood... the tape stops playing. I look down at the tape spewing out of the player, look back up and everything's in slow motion... I am spinning over and over, each spin seems to last too long as I await the crunch of steel on dirt... I can see the road approaching my head and flinch just as the driver's side hits the dirt and begins a long slow slide to a stop with my arm under it...

I wake up screaming.

I look around me in the darkness, totally disorientated, no awareness of where I am. After a while I can hear the beep of machines keeping people alive, and somebody snoring. I look at my arm, at the cage that surrounds it in case I try to smash it again, smash this mangled arm right off my body. *A hospital, I am in a hospital, but how the fuck did I get here?*

I drift back off to sleep.

Liquid Moments
19 years ago

I unwrap a dressing pack and get to work. I have done this so many times I have become an expert. Three times a day for 5 months now and still the infection is there, hanging on to my damaged arm like hot cheese to a cold knife, a constant reminder of the steel plate that runs the entire length of my lower arm, the cause of the infection. I carefully remove the bandage and the non-stick gauze underneath, revealing the small open wound amongst the moonscape of my arm. The skin grafts covering half of my arm look translucent; I can make out the veins running underneath.

From the kitchen table, I can see out the windows to the surrounding tree covered hills. In the foreground I can see the early sun illuminating the hothouse: the beans, snow peas, tomatoes, and strawberries will be loving this gentle hit of sun, before the mesmeric midday heat arrives. And it will, the last two days cracking 40 degrees, putting us on a knife edge both days, our noses in the air checking for the first whiff of smoke that signalled bushfire, bags packed and ready for a quick escape. But there is no quick escape when there is 5kms of thick bush between you and cleared, open ground.

When Em and I first came up here from Melbourne to check out this house, it was early autumn and we thought we had found some kind of

Eden. There were fruit trees laden, raspberries, corn, herbs, and the house... wow... 2 storey, 4 bedroom mud brick house, balconies off each end. One whole gable end had a huge leadlight feature, a multi-coloured tree with a leadlight bird and koala hanging off it, which you got to by going through the 'conversation pit'. Yep, we had arrived at hippy-ville and we were ready for it, ready to get out of the city and raise our soon to arrive daughter in a different place, in a different way, a conscious way, miles away from the voracious grasp of society. The cold war hadn't ended yet and I used to say to our inner city friends when they asked why we were leaving to go live in the sticks, that 'at least we will have a nice view as the orange flash hits and Melbourne burns'...

Thought I was so cool back then, so offhand about the threat of instant annihilation that we had spent our entire lives in.

That first year we grew lots of vegetables, collected our own firewood, pruned and harvested the fruit trees, tended the herbs... we loved it. I relished the physicality of it after many years of sitting around in the city reading Camus, Celine and the like, watching old movies and avoiding the world.

By the time we had endured our first winter in the bush, with a veil of insipid drizzle and low cloud for 3 months, we had started to understand why the owners had left and the rent was so cheap.

Eighty five acres of natural bushland, the house, 2 artists studios, a huge dam with an island in the middle with a majestic salmon gum tree towering above it... *fuck, it IS an Eden*, I think, *even in the early hours of another scorcher it seems a better option than a dump of a house in Melbourne for twice the rent.*

I return my attention back to my mangled arm as I hear the light steps of Cass gingerly negotiating the stairs. And finally, she does.

"Dadddddy!"

"Morning sweetheart, did you sleep well?"

She is standing at the foot of the stairs rubbing her eyes.

"Well Dad, it was funny cause I had this dream I was back inside Mum's tummy."

"Wow Cass, what was it like?"

"There's a green couch in there, Dad."

"What, in Mum's tummy?"

"Yes and it was so nice I fell asleep on it. Can I help, Daddy?"

"Yes of course, sweetheart."

I brush her wild wispy blond hair off her face with my good arm as she reaches across to the opened dressing pack and picks up the plastic tweezers to begin.

This had become a morning ritual for both of us these last few months and even though it was a grisly task, I had begun to look forward to it, to see the look of total concentration and compassion on my little girl's 3 year old face. Usually I would try to get a start before she came down so she didn't see how much green puss there actually was and she could do the final clean and re-bandage, her favourite task. Today I didn't get there.

"Daddy, why is your arm not getting better?"

"I think it's because of the steel plate holding my arm together."

"Why?"

"Um, I think my body doesn't like the steel and wants it to go away."

"So do I Daddy!"

"Yeah, me too."

She very gently picks up a piece of gauze with the tweezers, dips it in the saline solution I had put in one of the little plastic trays and gingerly dabs away at the small open wound between the stomach flap and the skin grafts. I gaze at her with a lump in my throat and as I blink a tear escapes and makes its way down my cheek.

Looking up at me Cass asks, "What's wrong Daddy?"

"Nothing sweetheart. Sometimes when I am really happy it makes me cry, you know?"

"You cry when you're happy??"

"Yeah, weird hey?"

Suddenly her dabbing and my squeezing produces a fresh gush of the foul smelling green puss which floods out past the gauze she is holding over it.

"Oh Dad, that's gross!"

Screwing up my face in disgust, I agree with her. Inside though, after all the various horrors of the last six months I seem to be numbed to it, almost like it was somebody else's arm now.

"Why did you crash the car, Daddy?"

I look outside to the smashed up car slumped in the carport, the smashed windscreen, the V-shaped dent in the driver's door arch and roof that was a daily, cold reminder of a moments stupidity.

"Daddy was driving too fast sweetie. I was being silly and I paid the price," looking at my arm. I thought of what the nurses had said: that with 2 crushed arteries, if the skin had broken when my arm went under the car, I would've bled to death in a matter of minutes.

I look up at my beautiful daughter and I see in that moment that I wasn't meant to die then, otherwise I would have.

She looks at me as if she has heard my thoughts.

"Daddy, I want you to get better. I don't want you to be sick anymore, I don't want you to die!"

I look down at my arm as Cass is wrapping the bandage very gently around it, and at that moment, for the first time, I see what I had done. I could finally feel the first blow, it wasn't slow-mo anymore, and I winced at the chilling reality of what was left of a good arm.

I look at my daughter and smile,

"OK, let's play the cup game Cassie, whaddya say?"

"Yeeeessss!"

She puts the cup on the table in front of me and I begin the slow and difficult task of trying to pick it up with my deadened hand, and failing...

Sledgehammer
40 years ago

The street has come alive, it seems like the whole neighbourhood is outside the front of their houses watching the spectacle. Nadia has put me down and is clasping my hand tight as we all stare across the street at my home. There is a naked light bulb swinging eerily in the lounge room as my father continues his mad siege, the last of the furniture coming out the window to join the broken remains of everything else. I look up at the adults around me. All of their expressions are the same, mouths agape, eyes wide open and a look of disbelief. Even the Sampson kids are there, one of them clutching her teddy bear and sucking her thumb, her eyes like saucers.

I can see my Mum's expression of wide-eyed terror as she stumbles down the front steps holding my sister, my two-year-old sister. And she is howling, a long shriek that cuts right through me. My brother is leading the way, looking purposefully ahead and focused on the task. He kicks the debris out of their path as he runs. I watch him scanning the approaching ground like it is the opposition on the footy field. He ducks and weaves around the broken chairs and the TV with a mixture of fear, determination and bewilderment etched into his seven-year-old face. My Mum is a few steps behind him, I can hear the scuff of her slippers on the driveway and can see her dress billowing with her hurried movement.

Craig straightens up and slows when he sees our car out in the street complete with a chain smoking red-eyed woman in the passenger seat... a moment later he looks across at the side mirror in the gutter a few feet from where I am standing, then looks up at me. I feel a smile spread across my face as I look back at him, knowing he has made the connection.

Suddenly there is the sound of cars coming up the street. I watch as the blue and red flashing lights bounce off all the houses, off all the faces of the dressing gowned neighbours, off the solitary white car, off the terrified face of my Mum as she stops momentarily, mesmerised by the lights. Down the street I can see that the police cars have slowed and Mr Barclay is pointing up the street to where we are.

As Craig approaches I can see him saying something to me but I can't seem to hear it, even though there are no sirens and the house has become strangely quiet. I can hear the buzz of the insects on the streetlights clearly, but nothing else...

A Beach in Thailand
Present

The waves hiss just like the insects buzzed around that streetlight 40 years ago. *I can still hear it, maybe I'll never stop hearing it* I think, as I watch another monster wave spread itself thin, like butter on warmed bread. *Have I been paralysed all this time? Am I waking up or falling asleep again? What the fuck is happening to me?*

The log, it seems, will not give in without a fight even though the waves have been increasing in size with each set. Its girth must be huge and mostly submerged, the various branches worn smooth by the ocean, the knotted growth caressed and softened so that it resembled some sort of sculpture... bobbing around in the water. Dancing with death it had been reshaped, altered, and yet something intrinsic to it had not changed, some deeper thing, some essence that the ocean could not dilute.

I can see many pieces of small driftwood around it, caught up in the waves and riding the crest onto the beach where they roll over a few times and then are laid to rest. A beautiful orange piece is flung up into the air as the wave breaks and falls down again into the foam. Submerged, then revealed, as the wave retreats back into the ocean.

A baby's flip-flop comes to a rest a few feet away. I stare at it and wonder what combination of circumstances delivered it here. It is pink and has been in the water a long time, partly eaten away by the sea, the remainder caressed and smoothed until it, too, looked sculptural. I picture a child in Bangladesh or Thailand or Burma or India losing one at the beach, I see the makeshift spade and bucket she is playing with, I imagine the hot sun beating down on her, the remonstrating parent as they watch it get carried away by the sea. And worse, I imagine a child's foot in it, falling off one of the many over-crowded refugee boats that fill these oceans around me. I picture a sea gypsy child throwing theirs away in disgust and running off down the beach, barefoot and laughing, feeling the first of many freedoms that no amount of Coca-Cola or iPhones can dispel...

I see my father's disgust wash up next, a turgid lump of sea-worm ridden wood that looked like it had lived forever out there, tossed around endlessly, a kind of hell. I see my mother's resolve land on top of it with a squelching sound, like standing on a snail. I see my father's hand as I mistakenly pick it up and kiss it thinking it was my sister's, I can hear his mocking laugh coming across the water as I sit, alone and smiling, the smile my brother saw all those years ago...

The Raffle
20 years ago

Finally the zookeepers allow me to get out of bed. When I stand up it is like that first joint ever, the head rush that I chased with every other joint after that. I have lost two stone out of ten. My legs are weak. I get to a wheelchair.

"Let's go Pete!"

"Where mate?"

"Outside onto the balcony. You can get out of bed, can't ya?"

"Yeah, it's just that I can't be fucked."

"Aah c'mon you useless bastard, get up!"

As I clumsily push myself along with my left arm a deep blast of pain envelopes my mangled arm and I realise it is the first time I have really moved it in over a month. Pete is also in a wheelchair but he is much better at it, having had years to practice and his fingerless stumps seem well suited to the task. He crashes into me on the way out dodgem car style and I laugh and wince at the same time.

Around us the ward is going about its business, the nurses cleaning the wounds and dispensing the drugs that, if they were lucky, will give them a moments respite from the madness just simmering below the surface of their patients... There is much coughing and spluttering, the beeping of the machines keeping some of us alive, and fuzzy announcements coming over the P.A.

I notice as we pass the Christmas tree that someone has added a pair of prosthetic arms and arranged them to look like the tree was jogging away. I stop in front of it and take it all in... the worn prosthetics, the Christmas hamper full of ham, biscuits, chocolate coated fruit, jars of jam... in short, all the things no-one here could eat. I laugh out loud. The tree is browning out and drooping severely after so much time around the sick and the dying, and I cannot help but feel the same...

Outside a vicious hot north wind has enveloped the city in a suffocating hold. Horns are blaring intermittently, a fire engine screams through the traffic on Royal Parade. Ambulances rush in and out of the hospital. I pull a joint out of my pocket that a friend had given me weeks ago, light up and pass it over to Pete, and look out from the 7th floor over towards the western suburbs.

"No thanks, I'm a juice man."

"Fuck, I'm not sure whether we're in the madhouse or they are," I say, staring out at the city.

"Yeah." He takes his flask out, gulps, coughs heavily for some time.

"That stuff is killing you, Pete."

He sighs and then grinned at me.

"Yeah, I know. Yeah, so one night Gordon and me are drinking and he gets up to find more wine and has a heart attack... mate, I loved that guy, he was in pain and I couldn't get to him," pointing to his lack of legs with his fingerless hands.

"So I crawled over to the phone and called here. Later at the hospital the doctors told me that he had survived, but one more drink will kill him. He hadn't told me about the cancer, the bastard. The first stop we made when he got out was the pub. He seemed alright, you know, sort of a strange yellow colour, but OK. The days rolled on. We got drunk for months. He told me he wanted his organs donated for medical research. They could pull him apart, he reckoned, to see what a 20-year drinking binge does to a man. Well, as sure as a runny shit he collapsed again, this time into a coma..."

"Mmmm, " I murmur. I try not to catch his eyes.

"I stayed by his bedside for a week. I loved that bloke. Then he woke up..."

Pete stares at the ground.

Just then the ward door opens and a bloke about my age, 24, comes out being held by two big orderlies. He is carrying a toilet bag under his arm. He looks across at us, says hello, and lights up a cigarette. The two orderlies light up as well and sit down either side of him. As he sits there smoking he looks straight at me. I return the gaze whilst taking long, luxurious pulls on the joint and smiling. He is still looking at me when he says,

"I know you. You done time?"

"No mate, " I reply, "think you've got the wrong bloke," turning to Pete with a 'what the fuck?' look.

Pete says, "Watch out for that one, he's fucking nuts, mate. There was a warrant out for him, the cops were chasing him at high speed when he crashed into another car, killing the mother and son inside it and also killed his wife and daughter who were with him. Fuckin' nuts that one."

I haven't taken my eyes off the guy with the orderlies as Pete is telling me this. Then the man yells,

"I fuckin' know you, mother fucker. I'm sure I met you in Pentridge. You're fuckin' Chris, aren't ya?"

"'Fraid not mate, you're barking up the wrong tree."

The orderlies have tensed up a bit on account of the raised voices and the fact that he is sitting up on the edge of his seat.

"You're Chris, I know it! Cheeky fucker, why you pretending you don't know me? You fuckin' owe me, for taking the beating that was meant for you! Remember?"

I turn back to Pete, shaking my head in disbelief as the orderlies push him roughly back down in his seat and then he is quiet, at last.

Pete continues his story.

"Gordon said to me, 'Pete me little mate, don't ever leave me.' I said I wouldn't, but a bloke needs to piss occasionally. He laughed."

Out of the corner of my eye I see movement, look across just in time to see the man leap over the balcony, his gown cord being the last thing I see go over. Pete looks across at the orderlies, who are now up and rushing about, then across at me.

"What the...?" I yell.

Dryly, Pete says, "That's the second one this week."

I am stunned, like a rabbit in the headlights. I hear the body hit, making a sound halfway between a thud and a squelch as it slams into the hard concrete.

"So anyway," Pete continues, "Gordon looks across at me, past the drips and machines, and starts talking to his dog. We're in the hospital, mate. He's patting the dog, talking gently to her, soothing her."

My eyes are burning, my ears ringing.

"He turns to me and says, 'Pete, me little mate, do us a favour will ya?' I say 'Yeah, Gordy, anything you want'. 'Pete, turn on the telly, I think I'd like to watch Bonanza'. I pretended to turn on the imaginary TV. He then said, 'Thanks, me little mate' and died…"

Pete holds his skeletal face in his fingerless hands and weeps.

I look at him for a long time, then out at the western suburbs. A huge black storm cloud hangs over it like a huge shroud. *Bonanza,* I think, *I wonder what his favourite episode was?*

I can hear the balcony doors being flung wide open.

Did that guy just jump or am I still in bed, dreaming this?

The screams from below bounce off the high walls all around us, careering up and out to join the crows as they circle the chimney, squawking in anticipation of another free meal.

Around us on the balcony the panic-stricken hospital staff try to deal with the suicide and its aftermath.

They take us back inside.

Liquid Moments
18 years ago

We are walking down the chilly Melbourne street. Cass is holding my hand and I am carrying young Han in the other arm. Cass has worked out how to hold this strange, twisted claw that I have had now for a few years. I look at her tiny hand clasped around my thumb, the only digit that looks and feels right, and I guess it makes her feel like everything is OK, back to normal as we walk towards the hospital entrance.

But everything is far from OK.

We stand on the corner of Nicholson and Victoria Street and wait for the 'green man' as Cass calls the walk signal underneath the traffic lights. Gusts of wind come down through the park and we huddle together to keep warm as we wait. Traffic is heavy and backed right up to Exhibition Street. Even though the light is green the cars are not moving. I look at the cars and their drivers, noticing that every single car has only the driver inside, all looking glum. They inch their way along the street as if that inch makes some kind of difference, some ending up in the middle of the intersection thereby blocking traffic in both directions. A light drizzle had started to fall, reminding me how much winter in Melbourne sucks and how good it feels when I have my hometown in the rear view mirror as I drive back to our house in the bush.

Cass is clutching the flowers she had picked for her Mum in her hand and looks confused as she stares out at the traffic. Her world was full of the sound of birds and the peaceful crackle of the bush. Fuck, we didn't even have a TV, and I wonder what she makes of all these people sitting dejectedly in their separate steel cocoons.

"Dad, where are these people going, they look sad..."

"I guess they're going home sweetheart."

"Then they should be happy shouldn't they Dad?"

"You'd think so."

"Then why aren't they?"

"I dunno, maybe they are in a funeral procession Cass, everyday they die a little bit more as everyday the noose gets pulled tighter..."

"You know Dad, a lot of the time I don't understand what you are saying!"

"Sorry, I forget you are only 5 sometimes... well, some people die fast and some die really slowly and these ones," looking at the cars, "are doing it the slow way."

"Is Mummy dying Daddy?" Hannah chirps in, direct as always, her dark brown pools of eyes boring into me.

I squeeze her instinctively and she wraps her 3-year-old legs even tighter around my waist. Cass is looking up at me in vulnerable hopefulness. I kneel down and pull her into a cuddle.

"Your Mum is sick girls and she IS going to get better and when she does we will all go home together," I promise. "Oh look, green man walking! Let's go!"

As we cross the street I can see Cass looking at the faces of the car drivers we walk past.

"I don't wanna die like them Dad," she says.

I get a flash of Cass as a 3-year-old, lying on her trampoline looking at the clouds and when I walk up to her and ask her what is wrong she says,

"Dad, how come everyone dies? I don't want to die. I am really sad that we all die."

I squeeze her hand now, just like I did then, look at the cars all lined up and reply,

"Me neither Cass, me neither."

I get a shiver when we walk through the entrance to the hospital. It's been two years since I have been in a hospital and the stench of disinfectant sends me back into the belly of the 7th floor Plastics ward, and I struggle to keep it together as we approach the lifts.

I have to be strong, for my girls' sake and for Em's sake.

I catch a glimpse of us in the shiny stainless steel lift fascia. I see my long, dirty hair under an old op-shop hat and my scrappy beard and the wild look in my eyes. Two years of binging is starting to leave a mark on my young face.

Fuck, I look 40.

I see my girls in their good dresses and wool leggings, scarves and beanies watching each number light up as the lift approaches. Cass is sucking her thumb and Hannah is buried in my coat clinging tightly to me. Terrified, I look at us as I wonder if I will be raising our children by myself...

Hannah squirms out of my hold, joins her sister and they run towards Em shrieking, "Muuummy!" in unison. A nurse stops me and, by the look on her face I realise I must look like shit. I hear her asking,

"Can I help you?"

She looks at me disgustedly as I realise that without my girls by my side to legitimise me I was naked, to her I looked like a lunatic on the edge of an episode, a bum, a hippy... the enemy, when all I really was, was a guy who had the lid peeled off his life and decided he didn't like what he saw.

The last two years had gone by in a blur of drugs and alcohol as I struggled with all that had happened to me. I had given up on rehab and opted to just get out of it instead and give in to the ever-present shadowy lure of despair. It seemed to be all the rage; the bars and remote, broken down houses I was hanging out in seemed to be full of like-minded souls. They called me Freddy Kruger on account of the old man's hat I wore and the strange machine strapped to my damaged arm with 4 long plastic tines connected to my crooked fingers, continually pushing my fingers straight, then pulling them back again. The whir of the little motor was my constant companion for some months. After a while it had an almost comforting regularity about it, and so did all my fucked up party friends...

"Nah, I'm 'right thanks." I eventually reply, giving her a big smile as I make moves to go past her. She reluctantly steps aside, saying,

"It's not visiting hours, you know."

"Yeah I know." I pause and then say, "And I don't give a fuck!"

The colour drains from my face when I reach Em's bed. There are tubes going in and out of her, she is crying as she smells the flowers Cass is holding up to her nose. Her face is drawn tight as I kiss her forehead and I can feel her face relax for an instant when my lips touch it. She looks totally exhausted, her eyes sunken and pinned from the painkillers, making her look lost and faraway from this bed, this hospital, this operation that just removed her large bowel.

Hannah is trying to climb up on the bed and Cass is stroking her Mum's hand. Em looks pleadingly at me and then her body tenses up into a ball of pain and a howl comes out of her mouth that is like a fist to the face, it being filled with such desperateness. I grab Han.

"Tone," she gasps, "get someone, this painkiller isn't working. Get someone!"

I yell to a nearby nurse and she walks briskly over, closing the curtains on the way.

"Dad, what's happening, what's wrong with Mummy?" Cass is crying and looking terrified.

I pick her up and take them both out into the ward. I can hear Em's screams getting louder and they are cutting through me like shards of glass. I am holding both the girls as they howl with their Mum, their faces terrified by the sounds. I look at another nurse and gesture towards my children as if to say, 'can you look after them and get them out of here?' She nods and we take them into the office, shut the door and suddenly the howls of pain are a distant thing.

"Girls," I say, "Nurse Tanya here," looking at her name tag, "is going to play 'office' with you, OK? Dad has to go help Mum, OK girls?"

"But Dad," Han sobs, "I don't want you to leave!"

"I won't be long, girls, OK?"

As I go out the door I can hear Nurse Tanya trying to calm them down, reassuring them that it will be OK.

As I enter the corridor I see a doctor going into Em's curtained-off bed and I rush in behind him. He looks flustered in the face of my wife's howls of anguish. He checks the machines then turns to her and says,

"Now calm down Emma, the machine is working, your pain relief is adequate and there shouldn't be a problem. Now, where does it hurt?"

"I just had my fucking bowel removed, where do you think?" Em spits through gritted teeth and looks at me incredulously.

I look hard at the doctor and say,

"She is obviously in pain, mate, now do your fucking job!"

He turns to me and says arrogantly,

"I'll have you know that I am the senior anaesthetist at this hospital and I do not make mistakes with my patient's pain relief. I even sighted this epidural myself! I'm afraid I can't turn it up anymore, it'll kill her," and then turns to Em and says,

"Now Emma, you're just going to have to be a bit stronger, the pain will go away soon."

And with that he walks out.

A look of sudden realisation lights Em's face as another spasm of pain hits her. She is pointing to her back and looking at me. I put my hand softly down on the bed next to her and slide it under her back. About half way there, my trembling hand hits a wet patch. A big wet patch. Em nods slightly and closes her eyes slowly as I rush out through the curtains to get the arrogant anaesthetist.

"Oi... YOU!" I yell at him, "FEEL THIS!"

I rush towards him and I thrust my hand out in front of his face. He flinches but not enough and my wet hand makes contact with his cheek.

"That, you arrogant fuck, is from under her back, that perfect epidural you sighted is leaking!"

I grab him by the arm and yell, "NOW FIX IT!"

He tries to shrug me off but I dig in tight and lead him towards the curtains and my screaming wife.

Within minutes he has rectified the problem and I watch with relief as Em slips slowly into sleep, her tense face relaxing with each wave of the painkiller. I start to breathe normally again, the pounding in my chest replaced by the dull throb of vengeance. I hear myself saying to him,

"I should fuckin' sue you, you prick!"

A smile gets started in the corners of his mouth, he looks me up and down as he says,

" I very much doubt you could afford that. She must have moved during the night, so it was her doing."

I see myself launching myself at him. I push him through the curtains onto the floor and then I am on him, punching him and shouting,

"YOU'LL JUST HAVE TO BE A BIT STRONGER... WHERE IS THE PAIN?"

And every time I hit him his face would transform... I was hitting my father, I was hitting my own stupidity, I was hitting all the people who had fallen asleep at the wheel and let an ordinary life erode their spirit. I was hitting the surgeon who loved concert pianists, I was hitting the cold morning light with a fist I couldn't even feel.

I stop abruptly and look at his bloodied face for a moment.

"Didn't even say sorry, did ya mate?"

As I raise my bloodied and throbbing hand above my head the orderlies jump me and then I am sliding across the floor, laughing...

A Desert and a Slide Guitar
4 years ago

I am outside the stage door smoking and looking up at the poppet head when the door opens and Harry steps out quietly, closing the door very slowly so the sound of it doesn't echo up the stairwell and bleed onto stage. He pulls an expression like a cartoon villain and slinks over towards me, looking this way and that... I smile and continue looking out into the dark car park, holding out the tobacco pouch he is sure to be wanting. He has a dressing gown on over his Bazza clothes. Following my gaze Harry asks,

"So what is that thing up there, Tone?"

"Uuhh, it's an old poppet head from a gold mine they moved up onto the hill so the tourists can see the whole spectacle of this city, take some photos and fuck off to somewhere far more interesting. Those boot camp fitness places use it a lot. They send their fat, red-faced customers up and down the stairs whilst yelling abuse at them from the ground and updating their Facebook statuses!"

Harry laughs heartily, then coughs as he expels the smoke, building up to a staccato lung rattle.

"Shit Harry, even your coughs are theatrical!"

He laughs again, this time slapping my leg with each lung rattle.

"You ever been up there, Tone?"

"Nope, views bad enough at street level..."

"What d'ya mean, Tone? This city is beautiful, all those Georgian and Victorian buildings, the park, the theatre, the whole arts precinct, all those antique shops, second hand bazaars, the bookshops, don't forget the bookshops, Tone."

"I guess you're right, maybe I've just been here too long…"

"Of that there is no doubt, my friend."

The muffled sound of 500 people laughing makes it way through the sub floor of the stage and spreads itself through the carriageway next to us. I look out at the car park, at the hundreds of cars sitting idly whilst their owners are inside the theatre being entertained, and say to Harry,

"I love wandering around the outside of the theatre when a show is on, it makes it kind of surreal, like it's all happening in a vacuum, know what I mean? It's like the building is alive somehow, breathing."

"Aah that is my world, Tone. I am the dark that makes the light 'light'. I am the Bazza baring his guts on a stage AND the nervous fucker in the dressing room mirror wishing the blurry figure in front of him would take shape. They do breathe, these buildings, they have a spirit that is the combined artifice of every show that has come through here, every soliloquy, every musical number seeps into the woodwork and I feel like a baby at his mother's breast every time I walk into one… my senses tingle more on stage than anywhere else, it's more real to me than anything out there," he says, pointing to the car park and beyond.

"So which one is the 'real', Tone, see what I mean? Reality is just an illusion agreed upon by lots of people and the weird thing is that everyone's experience of that 'reality' is unique. It's a wonder they're all not as insane as we are..."

He lays back against the bench seat and says,

"You and I, my friend, live on the edge of both. We are fringe dwellers at a masquerade ball..."

He looks up at the poppet head and says,

"So you've never been up there? Well let's go then!"

"But what about the show, Harry? Aren't you meant to be up there, acting and stuff?"

"Got 15 minutes before I'm on again..."

"OK, then I'll show you a better view!"

I take him through the labyrinth of backstage doorways to the foot of an old timber ladder. We climb up into the sub-floor of the stage and creep quietly underneath the action, the stage floor creaking underneath the action as Wazza and the German backpacker sit at a bar telling each other about this crazy old guy who had picked them up hitchhiking.

We reach the fly system and cautiously make our way through the ropes and blocks to a little doorway that leads us into one of the exit stairwells. Harry's dressing gown cord keeps getting caught on old nails and cables until I see him shoving it roughly into his gown pocket. Up two flights of stairs and past the stacks of replacement theatre seats that are scattered up the last flight of stairs and then we are at the foot of another old rickety ladder, the final ascent to the roof.

I go first so I can pop the cover off with my shoulder. Harry isn't far behind. I can feel his weight on the rings of the ladder as he clambers up. I climb up on the roof and hold the ladder firmly so that Harry's antics don't kill him as I watch him climbing like an exasperated monkey with a balance problem.

When he pops his head up through the hole I am already perched up on the very top point of the building. Immediately below me is a massive stone feature of a lion's head with an old mouldy patina and below that, a 20 metre drop to the portico, eerily empty, with massive lights swinging gently on long chains in the night breeze. I gesture for him to come and join me.

"Don't walk on the slate, cause you might go through it!"

"Thanks for the tip, Tone!"

He gingerly walks across to me as I say,

"They bought all this slate for this roof from Wales when one of the best slate mines in the world was 30 kilometres away! Fuckin' weird, hey?" looking across at the vast roof of the theatre.

Once he is climbing up the façade I move to one side of the lion's head and Harry takes the other. Harry looks pale when he gets to me.

"You alright?"

Catching his breath, "Yeah, think so."

"Now this is the best view in town I reckon. Up high with a lion's head between your legs!"

Harry looks out, saying "Wow," and "Fucking wow!" as he takes it all in: the tree-lined arts precinct street in our foreground and the sprawling suburban nightmare going over the horizon. You can see the lights from the active gold mine on the outskirts of town, you can see the dull, empty city centre, you can see the hotted up cars loaded with drunken boys doing circuits of the nightclub streets, full of bravado fuelled by the urgings of their mates, you can hear the excited clicks of heels as girls make their way down to the nightclub slaughterhouses, you can hear the nothingness all around us. And yet it looks pretty good from up here, the old slate rooves of the old buildings, neo-gothic iron work ringing many of them, running around their edges like playful children.

I turn to Harry. Tears are glistening as they roll down his cheeks.

"You alright, Harry?"

There is quite a long silence before he answers.

"Tone, I feel FUCKING FANTASTIC!" yelling into the dark night.

The Release
6 years ago

I drop my right knee off the tank as I lean the Duke into the corner. I am crouched over the tank and Lisa is wrapped around me, her long legs squeezing mine. As the road comes up to meet us I give the throttle a squirt and the back wheel starts to slide, the hot rubber depositing itself in our wake. I raise my feet back off the pegs as I hear them scraping the hot tar and realise I should back off a bit, but soon enough we are through the corner and looking down a long stretch of straight road, a tunnel of overhanging trees above our heads. I ease off the throttle and sit upright, reflecting on how fucking alive this shit makes me feel.

Lisa puts her hands playfully over my visor and for an instant I cannot see. And it doesn't matter. In fact, I laugh inside the helmet and it echoes for a short time, the sound seemingly going back into my ears, over and over, and in the background the seductive, staccato rumble of the hot Italian engine.

The road ahead climbs a small hill and winds off to the left, more corners approaching us, a million thoughts racing through my head in time with the beat of the engine.

Suddenly I am on another corner years ago and my friend Totto is in front of me, the howl of his Ducati 1978 900ss beckoning me to go faster, to catch him. I can see his helmeted face now in front of me as

I ride with my girl through the Central Victorian landscape near my home.

***

Totto unclips his helmet and has a cigarette in his mouth and lit before I have pulled my terrified face from mine.

"You have to know your bike like your lover's body, all the moans and groans, all the sighs. Even the ugly moods, my friend, and then you can let yourself go and fucking ride that thing like this is your last moment on this tortured planet..."

He takes a drag on his cigarette and looks across at his bike, which is creaking every second or so as the engine cools.

"Fuck, man, I'm just trying to keep it upright most of the time. Is everything like a woman for Argentinians...?"

He laughs.

"You'll see Tone, you'll see..."

But I couldn't. A year before this I hadn't even ridden a bike before and now I was leaning beautiful Italian moving sculptures harder and harder into corners and trying to catch up to him, something I was yet to do.

I had met Totto at Uni when I was 17 and he was 25. He was the first man that I could look up to, he had an acid wit, an active mind, had travelled a lot and lived in all sorts of places. When he talked with his Latin accent he threw his hands around a lot and everything seemed to be a passionate experience. He had tasted life and he described the taste to me. It was all I had to go on at the time...

My first lesson was eventful, to say the least. We were at a party somewhere in Melbourne smoking hash and getting hammered on Vodka when one of the stoners around the kitchen table mentioned he had a bike for sale. Through the haze I hear myself asking to check it out and Totto asking for details, and it seems like only minutes later and I am sitting on it, swaying with the vodka and strangely vacant from the hash. I can hear Totto giggling with his girlfriend as he says,

"OK man, this one's the throttle, here's the clutch and the gears are down there," pointing vaguely towards my left foot. "OK, off you go!"

I am in the driveway facing the road, which is filled with parked cars. I rev the motor, pull the clutch lever and clunk it into first gear.

"Here goes," I say.

Totto is laughing still and I can hear him saying,

"Give it some gas!"

So I let the clutch out and I am off, the bike flying down the driveway, across the road and straight into my own car...

***

Lisa holds me tight as the next corner approaches. Her body becomes weightless against mine as I ease off the throttle a touch and we kind of float towards the apex of the corner. And then I see Totto in front of me again, the fat rear tyre of his Duke at 45 degrees to the road and mine following. I am not far behind him now and a new looseness fills my body as I twist the throttle hard and fly past him mid-corner, on the wrong side of the road. I glance in the mirror and I can see his face, it is a mixture of joy and suffering and he is smiling...

As we ride down the driveway towards the studio I realise I have no memory of the last 5 kilometres of highway, Lisa is hugging me from behind and has crept down the seat and I can feel her warm crotch against my arse. I ease the Duke to a stop inside the studio and cut the motor. I look around as Lisa dismounts and I can hear her leathers squeaking and her boots making contact with the ground. I reach for my helmet clasp and fumble with the thing whilst watching Lisa in the side mirror taking off her helmet and releasing her flame red hair, it cascading down her olive green leather shoulders. My fumbling succeeds and my helmet is now off as I take her in, her long legs in green leather going on forever, down, down to her retro boots. Her huge green eyes are looking at me. She looks like some kind of tiger as she walks towards me, slowly swinging her hips.

"Baby, you rode beautifully but now I'm all hot," unzipping her jacket as she walks, "I need to get out of these clothes."

We kiss long and passionately, her tongue swirling slowly around mine, playing with it like a cat with a soon to be dismembered lizard. I am running my hands up and down her leather clad body and squeezing her hips and as I do I realise I haven't put the bike on the centre stand and it is teetering dangerously to the side. I stop kissing and look at her.

"It feels fucking great to be alive! The closer I get to that tar, the more alive I feel," silently thanking Totto for introducing me to what has become a lifelong passion for motorcycles.

I climb off the bike and put it on the centre stand. Then I gently sit Lisa down on the seat and remove her jacket. Underneath is one of those rockabilly chick t-shirts. It is tight and I pull it up and over her breasts and feast on her flat, tight belly. She tilts her head back and leans back over the tank, putting a foot either side on the foot pegs and arching her back. The hot motor underneath us warms the flesh under my touch. She is moaning now and I release her breasts from her bra and watch the nipples go hard. I flick a nipple a few times and squeeze it between my fingers, which makes her arch her back even more. I put my arm under her back and feel the raised, rough skin of her new tattoo, a huge phoenix, then run my hand down and around to her zip for her pants. She puts her finger in her mouth and bites on it as I undo the zip ever so slowly and then ease her pants down her long legs. She lifts one leg at a time to help me. Pointing her toes in the air as each boot is flung off and tossed dramatically across the slate floor.

"I can't believe this... I must be dreaming!" I say.

She is rubbing herself through her panties with one hand and holding the handlebar with the other and replies,

"Come here, dreamy man..."

I turn her over and watch the phoenix dance on her back...

The Release
2 years ago

I throw another pile of rubbish into the trailer and look across at the studio. How long ago was it that our wails of pleasure seeped out through the doors and down the dry valley? I stare at the Duke sitting in there, waiting to come alive on a highway somewhere. But I don't seem to have the time anymore, or the inclination.

The judge had made his decision, I had refinanced my mortgage for the second time to pay her out and was now free to finish the house and fuck off out of here, release myself from the horrific drudgery of paying a mortgage on a house I could never own now, unless I worked for another 30 years. The dream house I had built with my own hands for next to nothing was now a chain around my neck.

I collect all the carefully placed 'debris', throw 90 per cent of it in the trailer ready for the rubbish dump, and make a big pile out of the rest. The frill - necked lizard with the ride–on mower in its belly had stayed and had been joined by many other surreal sculptures, testimony to many a drunken solitary night. I had begun paving the verandas and had spent every spare moment collecting the slate and then laying it crazy style. I had emptied every room in the house except for one and they were in various stages of being painted again, this time a neutral off-white that I was hoping would have a nice effect on any potential buyers. If I kept busy, paving on days off and painting of a night time after work with music pumping and a drink nearby, then I wouldn't get buried by all the memories these walls absorbed like water to a dry sponge. I wouldn't get trapped in that cycle of despair and cynicism that I had seen so many other men fall into.

I had become allergic to commitment, to those words that can imprison a couple without their knowledge of it. I had retreated even more from the world, lucky to see one human being on my days off. And I was starting to like it.

On most Sundays Cass and Hannah would come over, arriving in their pyjamas, hung over from nightclubbing and they would search out my couch, where they would doze and we would watch movies, sometimes one after the other, until we were so image-saturated that we couldn't take anymore. I would cook a roast meal, stoke the fire and watch them sleep, my 20–something daughters asleep together on my couch, like all those years ago…

I throw an old child's cot onto the growing pile. The autumn sun had lost its warmth hours ago and has been shamefully retreating ever since. In the distance I can see the power lines illuminated a golden colour so that they resembled Christmas ribbon wrapped around a present. I pick up a handful of dry eucalyptus leaves and shove them in under the pile, pull out my lighter and wait for the crackle and hiss of the oil-laden leaves igniting. Within minutes the bonfire is a 10 metre high wall of orange flames, putting the old bed in a fiery silhouette. I am sitting watching it burn, watching my bizarre sculptures being thrown into a soft amber light, sending eerie shadows around the place as the wind dances with the fire.

141

Years of accumulated stuff... old rotten doors, window frames that 'might come in handy one day', fucked-up cheap furniture that had been given to us or had bought from an op-shop, half baked projects that never got off the ground, old doll's houses, defunct chairs I was going to repair one day, even some of the tortured mistletoe branches went into the fire. By the time the fire is peaking the last of the light has disappeared and I become mesmerised by the flames a few feet away from me. So many years seemed to have gone past so quickly, only yesterday I was putting Han down to sleep in the cot that is now engulfed in flames, the paint peeling away and floating up and off with the smoke.

There is no time except now, I say to the flames.

I watch a piece of 'mistletoe' burning, the flames forming an orange shroud around it; its demented shape exposed one last time. I pick up another to throw on, the shaft seems to fit snugly in my hand so I stop mid-throw and look at it, holding it up to the fire. It has a shaft of beautifully aged grey wood, finishing in a big twisted root ball. It is about three feet long... I look at the root ball and at first it doesn't seem remarkable. I look closer and just then an old box explodes in the fire throwing an almost white light onto the root ball and I can just make out the shape of what looks like a face screaming. I get up and kneel close to the fire, turning the piece around and around. There's not just one face, there are hundreds of them all clustered together to form the twisted ball. It looks like Munch's 'The Scream' embedded in the root ball of a small tree. I get lost for quite a while as I marvel at this amazing thing I was about to burn. A whole city of screaming, skeletal faces, a city of lost souls...

I watch the fire burn out, holding onto the mistletoe the whole time. When I finally go inside I place it on the large, empty table in the kitchen, sit down with sandpaper and a chisel and start work. There is not much to do; it is already perfect. I decide that I will mount it and put it dead centre of this table. I look around my big, empty, silent house, which is mostly in darkness. I look at the city of lost souls as it reveals itself to me and I smile when I realise that this chain around my neck will also be the thing that saves me.

A Beach in Thailand
Present

The high tide has taken away nearly all the
beach and I can see Phee Noi and Phee Nan sitting on
a log way off in the distance, waiting it out. In an hour
the sand will be exposed again as the tide retreats,
and so will all the treasures that we seek: the
discarded broken pieces of boats, the branches that
the ocean's caress has transformed into things of
extraordinary beauty. My lost log rolls almost
triumphantly just behind the break, it rolls up the
wall of each wave and is flung backwards as it passes
by. The early sun now hits the breaking waves
straight on, turning them a light green just before
each one crashes on the beach... I raise my hand to my
face and feel the lines etched deeply there, I feel the
ridges of my brow, the crow's feet trying to drag my
eyes apart. My 4-day growth is a fuzzy, grey blur. My
short hair is standing straight up, my eyes are puffy
and red from crying... I run my hand down my face
feeling the rough contours, the marks of my life. They
feel alien somehow, like some sort of weird stage
make-up applied hurriedly in the dark. I start
pressing my fingers into my face, it seems to move
and change shape easily. Soon I am pushing and
rolling my elastic face from one side to the other. I am
laughing from underneath the pudgy layer, but my
crow's feet don't come to the party, remaining visible

despite the latex layer. I push some of the layer down to my chin and push a dimple into it.

"*Kirk Douglas, eat your heart out!*" I mutter.

The brow is next. I push some of my cheeks up above my eyebrows and mould a Neanderthal shaped ridge. And now for the nose. I make a fist and wack my nose hard, squashing it across my face, then I twist the nostrils up like a pig's, giving me an expectant look. I pull at my lips until they stretch out and hang slackly down on Kirk's chin. The ears take the longest of all, a few minutes of manipulation and they are five times their normal size. I am in hysterics now, rocking back and forth on the wet sand, sinking more with each rock, smiling wildly through my distorted face, shaking my head from side to side, feeling my massive ears slap my cheeks... and the waves rushing up around me.

Sledgehammer
40 years ago

My father is standing there in the window, dead still and silent and smiling as the police lights fill the empty, wrecked house around him. Both cars come to a stop facing the white car, bathing the shocked inhabitant in the cold, white headlights. The first cop gets out of the car and looks around at the carnage out on the street, stuck in shrubs and lying forlornly in the driveway, shakes his head then moves his attention to the woman in the car. She is crying and trying to stub out a cigarette in an overflowing ashtray and failing, spraying herself in small, red coals. Howls of frustration join her sobbing. The cop seems unaffected, then turns his attention to my Mum, heaving and wild-eyed a few metres in front of him. She hasn't moved since she saw the lights.

The other two cops are heading towards the house. My father is still just standing there, looking out at them and smiling. Now he is casually swinging the sledgehammer back and forth in his right hand and pushing the hair off his face with the other.

The first cop is talking to my Mum, who is trying to rock my sister off to sleep and tell the cop what's happening. My brother is holding my hand and we both watch as the teddy bear my sister is holding slips from her grasp and falls to the ground. I stare at it on the ground, bathed in blue/red lights. No one else seems to have noticed – my sister is oblivious as she drops her head on my Mum's chest and sleeps. My Mum turns towards my brother and I, pointing with her chin. The cop nods and says something to her. She nods and starts walking towards us.

Suddenly the sledgehammer starts up again, my father is laughing and smashing anything in his path now. The cops are at the bottom of the steps to the front door, bracing themselves for the madman inside as another coffee table flies through the front window. The cops run up the steps, kicking the door open and with batons raised, enter the arena. Through the broken window I can see that my father has heard their approach as he turns and runs off in the other direction.

I can see both cops through the window now as they negotiate the debris-strewn house, chasing my father. My Mum has got to us and her fear infects us both, my brother's eyes dart around and I squeeze his hand, tight. I don't want him to let go, ever...

My Mum is saying something to us, then my brother is yanking me back off the street and into the Sampson's house. We all scurry down their driveway: Nadia, my Mum and sister, my brother and I. I turn around and look back at the scene: the neighbours, the flashing lights; the sounds of a scuffle coming from the house; the scared woman in the white car; the insects dropping from the light to their death, surrounding a forgotten teddy bear in the middle of the street with their spent carcasses...

Liquid Moments
11 years ago

Hannah comes rushing out the door and bounds up to me.

"Daaaddd, what're you doing?"

I put the trowel down on the freshly laid stone and say,

"Weeeelllll, I'm building a stone wall so Mummy can grow all her herbs, and we'll have an extra place to sit," looking along the curving line of the rock wall, noticing the pleasing way it seemed to emerge from the ground, the curve starting at ground level and increasing in height as the land falls away from it, until it is 2 foot high and kidney shaped.

"How come it's not straight, Dad, like it's all curvy and that?"

"Guess I'm not real straight myself, so the wall didn't have a chance!"

She laughs.

"Dad I was wondering something..."

I ready myself for one of a thousand razor sharp insights. Wiping the concrete off my hands seems to help. She is looking out at the front yard when I say,

"What darling?"

"Well Dad, you know how we used to have Dook's motorbike and we made all those jumps and I used to ride 'round the house really fast?"

I look at the place where we had built the biggest jump, big enough for her to leave the ground most times and come crashing down, nine times out of ten the bike and her separating in mid air.

"Yeah, that was fun, hey?" smiling at her. Her face is serious. I notice her hair is pulled back tightly into a ponytail with some sort of hair gunk holding it down.

"How old was I Dad?"

"Well, let's see. You're 9 now... I reckon about 7."

"Yeah, well I miss it, Dad, and I was wondering, am I old enough to have a go at the flying-white-bucket-of-shit?" pointing to my old car under the trees near the studio.

The girls both came up with the name one day when they noticed the holes in the seat, the window that disappeared into the door frame if you were silly enough to try and wind it down, the side mirror that flapped precariously on only one screw, the cracked windscreen, the collection of small random rocks that rolled around on the floor, the car stereo with the fencing wire holding it place, the layers of dust that flew up in the air when we went over a bump. It was nothing like their friends' cars at all...

"I guess we'll have to do the telephone book test then, and find out!"

"I'll go get 'em," she blurts as she flies off towards the house.

I put the huge telephone books on the driver's seat, move the seat as far forward as it goes, then say,

"OK! Let's give it a try!"

She climbs quickly up onto the books and stretches her body out, saying,

"Look Dad, I can see over the wheel now," turning the wheel around like she was driving it already.

"And I can reach the pedals too, Daddy!" extending her right leg as far as it will go.

I look concerned, but a smile starts to form as she pleads,

"Pleeeeaaase Daddy?"

My face is serious when I say,

"OK sweetheart, I think you're ready!"

"Yippee!" she squeals and reaches for the ignition.

"Hold on sweetie, Dad has to get in the car first!"

I am fastening my seat belt and about to say..."start... the", when the engine roars to life, Han revving the motor over and over. She's got her hand on the gear stick and her foot is depressing the clutch before I even have time to explain, redundantly it seems, what combination of actions will get us moving.

"OK sweetheart, pop it into first gear and..."

She slams it into gear, lets the handbrake off, drops the clutch and suddenly we are moving. The rear tyres have lost grip already and the gravel in the driveway is flying out behind us as she steers us towards the front gate, her face a contorted mixture of excitement and absolute calm.

She doesn't slow down to turn into the dirt road, rather she flings the car sideways, waits for the inertia to settle, then gives it more gas and leans forward over the steering wheel.

"OK, where to, Daddy?"

She shifts into second gear as I say,

"Straight Han, go straight!"

"Wow, Dad, this is fun, and pretty easy!"

We career up the road and where the road turns to the left we go straight, down a smaller dirt road. The rear of the car lifts slightly as we do, the car fishtails and did I just see her correct the fishtail by counter-steering? She has been driving for less than a minute and yet somehow the car responds obediently to her movements, almost as if she had done it before.

"So how long have you been sneaking off and driving my car, sweetheart?"

Silence. Just the whining of the motor and the sound of twigs being crushed under the tyres.

"Not long Dad, only done it a few times... and I always wear a seatbelt!"

"Jesus Han!" and then resigned, "but you seem to be a natural born driver, look at you go!"

She laughs, "The first time the car bunny-hopped down the driveway and then stalled, so I left it there, do you remember Dad, cause the car wasn't where you parked it?"

She slides it effortlessly into third gear and puts the foot down yet again as we approach the hill, the road winding tightly around the large trees scattered about. I reach up and grab the handle above the door and brace myself. Off to our left, a flock of cockatoos that had been feeding in the paddock next us take off in their anarchistic way, spraying our view with white and yellow flashes of feathers.

It seems like the trees are almost in the car as she swerves and then flips the car in the opposite direction, with just enough time to miss the next one, laughing to herself and humming a Spice Girls song.

"The second time we got it all the way down to the olive grove, then it took us half an hour to get it started, and boy, we were freaking out you were gonna go off at us, but then it started and we were like, phew!"

She swerves the car expertly through the trees, grazing the last one ever so slightly with the side of the car. I see the tree fly past my window, bark coming off it as we go.

"Um, can you slow down a bit, Han?"

"But Dad, it's fun, and besides I'm wearing a seatbelt and all the windows are up cause I don't want my arm to fly out the window like yours did."

My heart rises up in my throat as a series of quick images flash through my mind... the sound of metal sliding on dirt and rocks putting me right back there. Nine years ago. Hannah had just been born and if I had broken the skin that windy summer's day, she wouldn't have had a father and I wouldn't be here looking proudly at her as she gears down and manoeuvres around a large Yellowgum...

She isn't humming anymore when she says,

"You're really lucky you didn't die, aren't you Dad?"

I sit silently for a while and watch her gunning the motor as we approach the crest of the hill, hunched over the wheel, her eyes focussed firmly on the road ahead. *At this speed we'll leave the ground*, I think, and brace myself again.

Everything goes quiet as we sail through the air for a few moments before crashing back down onto the road. Han shrieks with delight as we hit and the flying-white-bucket-of-shit lurches on its springs and threatens to career off into the bush, but Han is having nothing of it, and as the road heads off to the right, she counter-steers the opposite way, neutralising the lurching and spearing the car through the narrow gap between two large trees.

"And the third time," Han continues, "we made it off our place and onto this road!"

She slows the car down, just letting the engine do the braking and then touches the actual brakes just at the end. The engine smells hot now as I hear her saying,

"Mmmmmm, I love that smell!"

I turn to her and she looks back at me, her eyes wide with adrenalin.

"Han, I think I better start taking the keys out of the flying-white-bucket-of-shit and hiding them," winking at her, "I gotta say, you've got guts, that's for sure!"

"I'm your daughter, Dad," she says, smiling at me.

"That you are darling, that you are. And let's hope you don't make the same mistake I did, thinking I knew how to drive, really drive, a car," looking at her pleadingly.

"The thing is, Han, just when you think you know how to do something, is when you should realise that you don't know much at all."

"Well that's your job, Dad, to teach me."

Just then the flock of cockatoos come up over the hill, surrounding the car as they fly spastically around, banging into each other and screeching loudly as they pass, a cacophony of mad screeches and, just like that, they are gone and are landing haphazardly in a nearby paddock.

"I guess it is, Han."

The Raffle
20 years ago

The large, light-blocking nurse is at my bedside, checking my stats and writing things in my file. She looks at me with a smile on her face and says,

"Well, Mr Cameron, it seems that they have managed to save your arm. The stomach flap has taken."

I slowly climb out of the grogginess of drug-induced sleep and look at her, then at my arm.

"Really?"

"Yep, looks like it. Yesterday's operation was a success: they have disconnected your arm from your stomach and, outside of a little infection, everything seems to be going well."

My arm is all wrapped up and has a cage around it. I try to twitch it and am relieved when a distant, dull throb of pain runs like deranged electricity through it. I wince as I try to sit up. My arm is in a sling and resting on a small trolley next to me. My stomach has bandages wrapped around it and has a raw feeling about it.

So do I.

"That's great, " I croak, but I can't seem to get excited about it. I feel like there is a thick piece of skin between me and the whole experience. The morphine wall that I have been climbing for 2 months makes everything seem distant to my touch and my fingers struggle to find a grip. I feel drained, exhausted, disconnected.

"Are you alright, Mr Cameron?"

I look at her with my well-rehearsed 'pained' expression, like I am internalising a nuclear explosion that will soon wrap itself around the whole world and vaporise it, if I don't get my shot.

"Pain's bad, sister!"

First she looks at me questioningly, then rolls her eyes and says,

"Well, OK."

Pointing to the file, she says,

"It says here that you are to have your pain management reviewed, but I guess I can give you one more course of pain relief."

I hated how they made it seem like I had to be a good boy or I wouldn't get dessert. *For fuck's sake*, I thought, *if only they could feel the pain for a second they would drop their moralistic tone and just do their fucking job.*

Even my veneer of indignation seemed plastic to me. I mean, how indignant can you be when you are shitting publicly into a steel bedpan?

I watch her put the needle into my drip and wait for the gorgeous warmth to flow through my body and when it does, I surrender to it. My eyes close slowly, I attempt to lick my lips with a dry tongue, I scratch my nose absently as I drift on the morphine cloud one last time. All the niggly aches and pains of lying in a hospital bed for months seem distant and insignificant now. My freshly scraped thighs stop burning, having been harvested for skin the previous day, skin that would be grafted onto my arm and stomach at some stage soon, they told me.

The nurse is still there watching me. I distract her with questions as I sense some urge behind her eyes, some need to say something that she has somehow contained… for now.

"When can I get out of bed? When do the skin grafts happen? Did they clean up the mess from the jumper?"

She retreats slowly, but not before telling me that, yes, I could get out of bed, and that the jumper went through the swimming pool roof and landed on the concrete next to the pool where a group of nurses were swimming… I pictured the stunned looks on the nurses' faces. The place that was a relaxing haven from death and illness had been sullied for them, forever.

As she leaves I drift off into velvet morphine bliss and I imagine holding my daughters in my arms again and listening to their stories and feeling them kick their legs against my waist, and with each kick my tears fall further down my face onto the stiff white smock I am wearing, soak through it, forming a stream down the middle of my chest, making their way slowly to the ground where my spirit is lying in a pool beneath my feet, tattered and bruised.

***

I wake to the sound of steel trays hitting the linoleum floor and as my eyes focus I can see my good arm raised and coming down on the bad one, making the trolley shake, making the walls moan, my laugh like a drunk ringmaster with nothing left to lose, a defeated triumph in it. I stop laughing when the first wave of bone-clenching pain hits me. I grimace and look up the corridor for the reassuring, stocking clad legs of a nurse, but to no avail. I can see the Christmas tree, now a pitiful attempt to take our minds off our pain, the prosthetics ironically being the only part not sagging. There's a scattering of brown pine needles on the floor around it and someone has scrawled, 'Fuck it, I'm outa here!' down one leg in red Texta. The angel on the very top has been replaced with a photo of a blonde chick in a 'Santa's Little Helper' outfit: short shorts, a fluffy top that almost covers her breasts, and thigh high boots. She is looking over her shoulder at the camera, whispering 'Shoosh', half bent over waiting to be spanked. Someone has wrapped bandages over the decorations and a bedpan is hanging miraculously off one of the sad branches, and there are numerous alcohol swabs clipped randomly over the whole thing. Boy, it seems to have been good therapy for us all. The staff apparently happy for us to have deformed it so much, graffitied it, made it ours.

Another stab of pain takes me back into the belly of my own nightmare and I reach for the buzzer that is connected to the nurse, who is connected to my morphine. Just then, Pete stirs in his bed diagonally opposite me, near the window. I can see his half body curled up in the foetal position and his head tilted back almost impossibly in the other direction. He looks in pain.

"You alright, mate?"

Pete looks across at me, holding his contorted position.

"Been better, mate. This fuckin' shattered hipbone of mine is cuttin' into me, fuck it!"

"Nurse is coming now, mate, I just buzzed her."

I notice that I have broken out in a sweat, I can see it glistening on the skinny arm holding the buzzer.

Eventually the nurse enters the room and I point to Pete in the corner, she nods, and then she is at his bed looking at the paralysed half man lying there. She heads out of the room and a minute later comes back with a small cup in her hand. She gives it to Pete, he thanks her, pops the pills and drinks the water she is offering him. He coughs and splutters, and then he is silent apart from the low whimper that escapes his clenched teeth.

She walks over to me. I seem to be shaking slightly all over when I say,

"Pain's bad nurse, can I have some morphine?"

"Afraid not, Mr Cameron, the doctors have asked that we stop giving you morphine and taper you off your pain relief," she hands me a little cup, "So here's some paracetamol, shouldn't be in much pain now anyway," she says.

I look at her incredulously.

"But that's like putting a band aid on this mess!" I say, nodding to my bandaged arm.

"Aah, FUCKING GREAT!" I shout sarcastically, "give me morphine every four hours for two FUCKING months and then say, 'oh dear, you seem to have a dependence' and just wrench me off the stuff? I've heard of cold turkey, but this is a hospital FOR FUCK'S SAKE!"

"Sorry Mr Cameron, there's nothing I can do."

"Yes there is. You can FUCK OFF!"

***

Later that night I get out of bed after many hours of writhing and sweating and twitching, a relentless soundtrack of thrash-metal on fast-forward spinning around in my head. I am crying, laughing, sweating, knowing everything and then knowing nothing, feeling my pain and then feeling nothing, nothing at all...

The corridor is nearly empty as I pace up and down, the ward almost silent. I can hear my heartbeat like it is coming through the P.A., and a woman's wails of pain in the distance, and the scuff, drag, scuff of my relentless footsteps. I am muttering to myself as if trying to convince myself of an obvious truth, so obvious that I just don't get it. Every time I pass the nurses' station I eye off the drugs cabinet, noticing that all the nurses carry a key for it. I extend my pacing to include the room with the wailer in it. She is an old, Italian lady and she has been screaming 'mama-mia' over and over for hours now, and with each wail her pain intensifies, the sound of it echoing through the whole ward – yet most seem oblivious in their drug induced slumber. An old man even snores in the bed next to her.

I watch the night nurse trying to console the poor woman but she is having none of it, swatting the nurse away with her flailing arms. She is holding her rosary beads and making the sign of the cross over and over. The nurse raises and then drops her shoulders as if resigned to this reality, this soundtrack of despair. I am slumped against the corridor wall sweating and shaking when she walks hurriedly past. I follow her to the nurse's station and watch her get out her key and open the drugs cabinet, rifling through the drawers until she finds what she is looking for. She grabs a syringe, a tray and a little vial in her left hand, locks the cabinet and heads back towards the old, Italian mama. I follow her back there and watch as she tries to restrain the old lady, but she cannot... She calls for reinforcements and they hold the old lady down, who is fighting like her life depends on it. The nurse plunges the needle in, the old lady screams one last time as the morphine courses through her body, her screams slowly becoming whimpers and strangled moans.

The morphine now has a hold on her and her body relaxes under it, she sobs quietly until sleep overtakes her and the ward returns to some kind of normality.

I resume my scuffing and dragging and thinking of the wailing Italian mama that somehow made it bearable for me, until the first light of the day pierces through the dull grey curtains. It is then that I drag my exhausted body back to my bed.

And sleep...

A Desert and a Slide Guitar
4 years ago

"You can't live everyday as if it's your last, Tone, 'cause it's so fucking exhausting. Believe me, I spent most of my 20's bouncing from one insane random moment to another and guess what? I hit 30 and I looked haunted, hungry and desperate. Like any addiction, your tolerance builds and then you need more and more each time…"

Harry is applying his make-up almost absentmindedly and he is looking at me through the dressing room mirrors. I notice that every second bulb has blown and I can see the shadow left in its place. It gives his face an uneven look. He raises an eyebrow and dabs away at the deep lines in his forehead, slowly making them larger than life, a clown-like caricature of a man on the edge.

"I mean, fuck, mate, I'm as mad as a meataxe! I courted my madness with Byron, Thomas, Beethoven and Rage Against the Machine, sleepless nights full of wonder and long bleak days of hopelessness… so full of life I couldn't even string a decent sentence together… and bored, I got so disgustingly bored by anyone who didn't share it…"

I am slouching across two chairs with my head against the brick wall. I can see down the corridor to dressing room 3 and I can hear the German backpacker doing her warm-ups, some kind of guttural primal therapy thing, harnessing her inner beast, I wasn't sure, but she sounded totally committed to it. I could just make out her movements, which seemed to consist of being on her haunches and shaking her head wildly from side to side. Maybe she was shaking the beast out of her? Giving birth to her character? Did she do this every night?

"I drank in art like water to a thirsty man. I often found myself in public art galleries staring in awe at great paintings and weeping quietly, so thankful that there was something that gave worth to our existence. Great art made music out of colour. I swear, Tone, sometimes I thought I could HEAR the painting! Like I said, mad as a cut snake!"

Bek walks into the dressing rooms talking into a two-way radio.

"OK, Rach, I guess we should get it fixed on the next day off... oh, hang on, we don't get a day off!"

She puts the two-way back on her belt and says to the room,

"Anyone for a cuppa?"

"And," Harry continues, not hearing Bek at all, "the more mashed up my senses got, the more it made sense..."

I shake my head at Bek, she nods and turns to Harry, gives him a big dramatic eye roll and heads off towards the primal screamer.

'Wazza' strides into the room, all pumped up and boisterous, holding out a hand to me as he makes his way to his chair.

"Hey Tone, what's up?"

"We are teetering on the edge of madness, a beautiful madness. There's no hope except to adopt it as a sane response to an insane situation!" I grin at him as I take his hand and give it a squeeze.

162

"O... K!" he says warily, and then, with positivity bursting out of him and climbing the walls around Harry's tired old face,

"Well, I'm feelin' bitchin' tonight, bro!"

He starts shaping up to his reflection, hunching his massive tattooed shoulders like sides of rump, ducking into and out of the mirror lights.

"Feel like I could do 15 rounds with Ali... and outdance him as well!"

He jabs at himself in the mirror, a huge smile on his face.

Harry continues, "And in the end, I realised it doesn't matter what you do or don't do, nothing matters at all, existentially of course," as he dabs at his war paint, his voice trailing off at the end.

"Spiritually, well that's another matter altogether... the art, the books, the films are the sounds of souls screaming amongst the voracious chaos of existence, it is the pristine moment of life expressed in a million different ways for a million different eyes. Some of them hit a universal chord in us all and we call that transcendental, or simply, TRUTH..."

"Positively bitchin'." Wazza weighs in.

Bek is coming back up the corridor leaving the primal screamer to her own devices, shaking her head as if to say, 'well, now I've seen it all' as 'Bazza's' girlfriend "Muriel" enters the room wearing sunglasses and a scarf around her head.

"Evenin' all," she says drearily and sits herself down in front of the mirrors. She gingerly takes off her sunglasses and squints as she is blasted by the 25 bulbs around her mirror.

"Aww shit! Can we... Bek! Can we turn most of these off, they're burnin' my retinas!"

"Well, what do you think the stage lights are going to do to you? Harden the fuck up!"

Jackie laughs and Bek gives her a hug from behind, asking, "Had a few wines last night, did we?"

To which Jackie replies,

"A couple, yeah." She looks defeatedly at the mirror.

Bek releases herself from the hug and says,

"I'll be back in a tick."

And sure enough a minute later she returns with a nice full glass of chardonnay.

Jackie smiles appreciatively as she takes a sip and I watch as the colour slowly returns to her cheeks and she looks, in a vaguely intrigued way, at herself in the mirror.

Harry is putting the final touches to the Bazza make-up, working on the crow's feet around his eyes, accentuating the lines so that they do start to appear like claws wrenching at the side of his face. For a few moments everyone is quiet as they apply their various disguises, as they bury themselves under a figment of the writer's imagination, as they dissolve themselves, distil themselves, leaving just a core part of them there. I watch Helga approach complete with blond plaited pigtails, short shorts, hiking boots and a pink singlet, walking like someone carrying a heavy load on their back. When she enters the room she takes a seat next to me and looks out at her three partners in crime adding their final touches... She slaps me on the leg and says,

"We're a weird bunch, aren't we Tone?"

I grin at her, "But somehow it just works..."

Liquid Moments
4 years ago

The steel is the colour of straw when I pull it out of the forge and start working it, slowly and methodically drawing the end out to a point. The hammer makes a low, dull thud sound echoing off the dry ground into the bush around me and I wonder what shape will reveal itself this time. I look over towards the house and see all the bent steel and gnarly mistletoe wrapped around the veranda posts. It is my demented response to the drought, this covering my house in a shroud of gothic beauty. The insect-like shape of the house lends itself easily to this, I muse, as I return my gaze to the hot steel in my hand. I roll it over and over whilst hitting the end slowly, transforming the cold, hard raw product into a tactile thing. I start to curl the end back on itself and a spiral starts to form. It is a perfectly round thing, and as I put it back in the forge I think,

And now it's time to mess it up...

Around me on the ground there are many deformed branches waiting to be suspended in the twisted steel shapes that are themselves making a sizable pile on the floor of the studio next to the Ducati. I stare at the bike, my senses tingling, and wonder if I will make time today to ride it, having gone over a month with a dwindling interest that I couldn't bring to reality. Too much to do, too many memories that no amount of insane riding would erase. Every time I looked at it I saw her on it, an expectant look on her face mixed with doubt. And doubt was the one thing you could never get on a bike feeling. It would expose you like a jealous sibling.

The dry, brown landscape crackles around me. *Fuck, this drought is in its 17th year*, I realise, *and I have never seen or known anything else out here.* The dam I had dug had never filled up, the olive grove I planted had never known vigorous growth, the native trees I had planted year after year resembled make-shift bonsais, or the bonsais of a madman, eaten away by a hundred insanely hungry rabbits. The garden beds around the house were reduced to mulched patches of yellow, forming a light fringe against the terracotta walls. I had been standing my dead branches up in place of plants as they died for a few months now, and to me they resembled skeletal puppets awaiting their moment on stage. The irony was that there was no stage, no performance for them. For now, anyway. My few visitors seemed slightly troubled by this, remarking that it looked like the house of a lunatic, all the dead and twisted, the deformed and demented collecting around me like diseased disciples. This sort of comment just egged me on, pushing me further into the exquisite gothic abyss. Pity I didn't have any goth friends, they would've loved it.

I pull the hot steel out of the forge and have started distorting the perfect spiral with the ball of the hammer when my phone rings, vibrating against my thigh from the inside pocket. I put the hammer down and reach into my pocket with a blackened hand. A number is on the screen I don't recognise and normally I don't answer these ones, but this time, for some reason, I do.

I watch the steel turning from yellow to red and resist the urge to smash it flat and give the phone my best deadpan 'hello'. I expect to hear the tell-tale click that means someone from a Mumbai call centre has rung 'looking to save me money on my electricity bill', but instead I hear the cheery voice of Kath, a friend of mine who now lives in Thailand.

"Hey Tone, what ya up to?"

I look around me at the piles of steel and wood.

"Kath! W... where are you?"

"Well, Noi and I are havin' a beer at your local. Fancy a couple of weary travellers payin' you a visit?"

"Aah for sure! Awesome Kath, I'll give you directions..."

" No need Tone, the barman's beat you to it!"

I laugh and hang up, thinking of the nuggety barman's directions.

"Roight, well after you've been to the bottle'o', turn left and crack the first stubby..."

***

Ten minutes later, their tyres are swishing over the stones in the driveway. They pull up in front of me at the studio. I reach down and switch off the fan and the forge is now silent. I have a smile from ear to ear as I see Kath and her boyfriend Noi in their car staring out at me. I watch her noticing the piles of steel and wood lying in wait on the ground at my feet. She shakes her head as she gets out of the car, saying,

"Someone's gone crazy since I last saw them!" arms out and coming in for the hug.

I hug her and smile at Noi, who is getting out of the car and hurriedly putting a coat and scarf on. It is a beautiful warm spring day.

"GONE crazy?" tasting the words like an exotic dish from an Asian street stall. We pull out of the hug and I 'sawat dee khrub' Noi and hold an arm out which he takes by the forearm and squeezes, Roman style.

"Man, it's good to see you guys. How long's it been, two, three years?"

"Long enough for you to have gone completely grey... look at you! Crazy old man!"

Kath is enjoying this, taking the piss out of me. It's a term of endearment in Australia, a show of affection. I run my hand through my matted, dirty hair, which is standing up as usual, and laugh.

"This is my mad scientist look, how's it working? Do I look intelligent AND mad?"

"Well, you've nailed the mad, that's for sure," Kath quips.

"We could stand here doing this all day, me feeding you lines. Should we add beer to the equation?" eyeing off the six-pack in Noi's hand.

"Is the Pope a Catholic?"

There's something about the sound of a stubby cap coming off that seems to instantly relax me. Must be a cultural thing, this hiss of relief as the beer tastes air again. Noi is having a spot of trouble with his but eventually the grimace of the uninitiated is replaced with a relieved look as he views the damage done to his hand and takes a small sip of beer. I gulp down mine as Kath asks me where Lisa is.

"Aaah... moved out a while back..."

"Oh."

"Anyway, let me show you around!" I say, not wanting to go into it.

Noi has wandered off towards the frill-necked lizard with the ride-on mower in his belly so we follow. As we get closer Kath says,

"Tone, got some news. Noi and I are getting married in February in Phuket, wanna come?"

I look at her in amazement.

"Fuck, why not?"

"Jesus Tone, it's bloody dry here," looking down at the dam, "that thing ever fill up?"

"Nope. And everything you plant dies, 'cept these of course, my little gothic dance with drought... these things fuckin' thrive in these conditions, the dryer, the more bleak it gets, the more they love it!"

"Tone, they're dead branches."

"Sssh," I whisper, "they don't know!"

"You've really lost it haven't ya Tone?" Kath elbows me.

"Or found it," I reply.

I walk over to Noi who is immersed in the detail of one of the mutant branches that make up part of the frill neck, his eyes wide with interest. I think of the time he took me on my first driftwood adventure, my first beach full of debris all those years ago, how we struggled under the load of wet treasures with a pounding ocean deafening us, how the Andaman sea resembled an angry, rancid soup, rendered thick and lumpy by all the logs, broken pieces of boats and plastic floating in it.

"Noi, Kath, feel like a walk down to the river?"

***

I have my hand on Noi's shoulder as we walk, Noi looking around him and asking questions about the land, the brown dryness that soaks the moisture from his skin, the sheep in bare paddocks with no shade, the disused train tracks that were our path to the river, the trees that hung forlornly over the highway as we cross it. To Noi it must have looked like a kind of nightmare, the exact opposite of his verdant tropical country.

When we make it to the river, it is how I thought it would be and the reason I hadn't walked down here in a long time… dry as a bone.

We scamper down the riverbank and start walking along the dry riverbed on rocks worn smooth by water, now dry and crusty, with weeds growing through the cracks. The river bed is full of dead trees that must have been submerged up until a few years ago, submerged for a long, long time. I knock on a passing tree trunk lying on its side and it sounds like it is made of stone. I notice the water worn smooth branches, their struggle for life finally succumbing to what was a watery grave… Kath is collecting the dead reeds and weaving them together and before long she is fashioning a rough sunhat, complete with fly repelling frayed ends which seem to be working, leaving myself and Noi to continue the unconscious, perpetual swatting they call the Aussie salute.

It is like walking through a graveyard for trees, so many of them lying on their sides, their dead roots up in the air looking like the last reach of a drowning man. Then I notice something, a broken section of tree root caught by the others, suspended in four places. I climb in under the tree to get a closer look. It had jumped out at me for some reason, there were so many other similar pieces like this, but this one had caught my eye. I carefully disentangle it from the others and hold it up to the sunlight. It is amazing, a shaft about as thick as my wrist twisting sensuously out into a series of small branches about three feet long… the water had worked like a determined sculptor, accentuating the twists and turns, smoothing out the rough, pointy roots, reducing them all to their essence. As I turn it around and around in my hand I begin to see it, see it for what it really is. It's a beaten, old, weathered man standing with his arms outstretched, a look of resilience on his face as each blow had hit him, as each lumpy bit of road had thrown him off his seat. And his arms are outstretched as if offering a tasty snack to a room full of drunks. Even though the outstretched hands leave him open and vulnerable, it is in his nature, it seems, to be perpetually offering himself, his spirit, to those around him. I sit down on the ground next to the tree and stare in awe.

What else can I do? If you close yourself down it's a long slow death. If you keep open and optimistic then you are bound for a life full of disappointments. Will everyone I let in rip me off?

I stare at the man as I spin him around and watch the sunlight blast different parts of him. I look at my friends, who are busy with their own discoveries. Noi, having plucked a long hollowed piece of wood up from the riverbed and slung it over his shoulder, is walking towards me. When he sees me he stops. I look up at him silhouetted by a low-slung sun as he says: "Nothing is accident, my friend..." and continues walking towards Kath.

He turns back and points to my man.

"You come here to find that. Life is simple if you let it..."

A Beach in Thailand
Present

I spit onto the sand at my feet and watch the tide wash it away.

Death is never far away, I reflect, *and nor is the chance to be reborn.*

It is the razor's edge that we perch on and then convince ourselves that the edge could not cut us, that somehow it had been dulled by time, rusted and pitted by the salt air.

Who am I kidding?

My razor is a chunk of tree with no soil to sustain it, completely lost and slippery. So slippery and unsteady that getting a foothold is impossible, rather you 'beach' yourself on it like an overfed walrus... My razor is worn smooth, rather than resist the relentless beating of the ocean, it has succumbed and let go. If only I could let things bounce off me then I probably wouldn't be sitting here on this beach with my heart in my hands, in some kind of stupor.

And yet in letting go the log has found the least resistance and even in the face of a powerful, angry ocean, it has somehow found more strength in surrender, an odd sense of victory in the face of almost certain defeat. It's the guy on death row whistling on the way to his execution, it's the stinking bravado with a nervous bead of sweat running down the cheek, it's the old man hobbling across the insanely busy Saigon street and not missing a beat.

It's the calm grin of the madman as they strap him down and connect the electrodes, it's in the dreams flickering behind the deadened eyes of defeated men, it's in the twist of the throttle mid corner as the road slips away from you, it's in the eyes of a small boy watching his life burn...

Saying Goodbye
9 years ago

It had been going bad for some time, longer than I cared to admit to, longer than either of us cared to admit to. It had become so dysfunctional that its very dysfunction was what was holding us together. It was all we had left.

Years had passed since we first met, since I moved into her house and the flirtation began. Every night she would come home from work smelling of garlic and flour and baked food, and I would pour her a stiff drink and then listen as she ran a bath, listen as I heard her peel off her clothes, listen as her naked body made contact with the steaming water, listen as she took a sip of her drink, usually tequila, and placed it back down on the edge of the bath noisily, the noise getting louder as the glass was slowly emptied. And then there would be silence, not even the sound of the water moving around that hot young body to arouse my senses. I would picture her lying there, eyes closed, alcohol swimming in her system, enjoying the stillness. Often I would ask her if she needed a top up and every time there would be a pause before she would reply, with a slight lilt, "No thanks," and it was all I could do to resist finding any excuse to walk in and surprise her, declare my desires and be done with it, be done with the coy teasing repartee we had developed. My almost total lack of experience stopped me many times, with my hand shaking as it reached for the doorknob, trying not to breath heavily and failing, rehearsing the lines I would use in my head and hoping I would have the balls to make the first move.

Luckily for both of us, for she was even shyer than me, the tequila finally broke the ice and before we knew it she was taking off her top, unclipping her bra and suggesting we have a bath whilst I struggled to stand with the hard-on straining against my second hand pants.

And now 15 years later I stand in the darkness next to my dog Tubba's freshly covered grave and listen to her wails of pain as she sits on the veranda with her sisters, drunk and howling like a lost dog in a storm.

How the fuck did we get to this?

Within two years of meeting her I was watching her give birth to the first of two beautiful daughters, and even though we were different people, it seemed to work somehow. We had a focus, a reason to make it work. And there was no way I was going to do a runner like my father and she knew it.

And then a series of tragedies befell us and we struggled under their load, we struggled for years, we drank our tears away, we blew smoke over the abyss forming between us. We threw all our energies into the two beautiful souls we had created together, and the more they shone the more light spilled onto the abyss.

First her mother dies a horrible death due to cancer in her bowel, a cancer that could have been removed had she not been so embarrassed and caught up in that Catholic guilt shit and gone to the doctor when the bleeding had started. I remember standing at her dying mother's bedside with this skeleton that was once a vibrant, active woman, doped up on morphine whilst Cass is being hurriedly christened so that she could 'see Cassie in heaven'. Totto and his wife Mary, Em's favourite of her four sisters, are there as well, looking lost and bewildered, pinned out of their skulls just to get by. I can picture the frilly dress Cass was wearing and the photo that commemorated this strange and sad moment.

A few months later I have my accident, so more hospital woes. Em watches me drift in and out of madness and burning agony whilst still grieving for her mother.

Within a year Em has bowel cancer, which we get onto early enough to stop it killing her, but not before it takes her entire large bowel with it. We have two children under four.

And the last blow was the worst and if nothing else, this is the reason I am sitting here weeping at my dog's grave, listening to my wife's howls echoing off the trees and down into the valley.

I remember it so clearly I can almost feel it, I can almost smell the fear and grief, and taste the bitterness that followed.

***

The air was thick with the last pollen of summer as I drove up the driveway home. I had been gone for 5 days, having scored some work at a music festival down on the coast and I was hanging out to see my family.

It had been a tough year, but we had gotten through. Em's cancer was gone and I had started getting work at last. My arm was a painful, deformed looking thing but I had regained 70% use of it.

When I pulled up I could see Em and Cass out on the grass, a pile of timber around them, a hammer in Cass's hand. They both turn at the sound of my car and Cass runs over screaming,

"Daddy, Daddy!" and leaps into my arms. I squeeze her tight and then put her down as she is squealing,

"Daddy, just in time! Guess what? We're building a cubby!" and runs off towards her Mum.

Em is feigning an interest in the timber as I approach, smiling at her. I hear myself saying,

"Hey Em," when she looks up with a half smile and says 'Hi' cagily.

I quickly turn my attention to Cass.

"Aren't you supposed to be at school Sweetie?"

"Yes Dad, but I'm sick, look, feel my glands."

I feel under her jaw for heat and swelling but find none.

"Besides Dad, you were coming home today!"

"Aah, so you pulled a sickie! That's my girl!"

I laugh and pull her into me, tickling her on the way. She squeals with delight and squirms out of my grasp. I drop onto my haunches like I am ready to pounce, which makes her face light up and then she is running off excitedly, looking over her shoulder as I lurch after her, which makes my face light up. I tackle her and we fall onto the grass laughing, staring up at the sky, me waiting for my head to stop spinning.

Em is saying something but I can't seem to hear it.

"What?" I ask, my ears still ringing after 5 long days doing sound.

"I think Totto is trying to contact you. We've had 6 phone calls since you've been gone and every time I answer it's Fausto, Totto's friend, asking, 'Antony, where is Antony?' I told him each time you weren't here and he would hang up."

"OK, Thanks."

"Now Tone," she is smiling playfully now, "do you reckon you could help us with our cubby?"

I roll over onto my stomach and take her in. Long strawberry blonde hair, its waves caught in the slightest of breezes, her large, expectant eyes, a slight playful pout on her full lips.

"Yeah, sure." *How can I resist?*

"I'll just grab a drink and get out of these clothes," looking down at the black T-shirt, black jeans and worn out Dr Martens that I've had on for days now. If I'd known what was about to happen, I would have rolled over and kissed her one last time.

I had the fridge door open and was peering inside when the phone rang. I picked it up and heard the familiar ISD international call tone and then,

"Antony? Antony?"

"Yep, it's me. Como sta, Fausto?"

"Please wait Antony, I get Totto."

Totto comes on the line.

"Hey my friend, how are you?' I wait for the echo of my voice to die and then I hear him crying, and then he is saying,

"Tone, my friend, there's something I need to tell you." He is sobbing. I am getting scared now.

"What's happened, my friend?"

"There's been an accident. Mary's... Mary's dead..."

The shock has made me rigid and I hear myself saying,

"But you loved each other so much!" And now I am crying, telling him I love him, that I am here for him.

"Can you do me a favour? Can you tell Em for me? I can't do that man, not now." I can feel the grief strangling him, suffocating him until there is just a

178

gentle sobbing to break the silence, this silence that has echoed through my life ever since, the wordless commitment we both made that day, the friendship that was forged at that moment. The same moment that spelt disaster for Em, disaster for us all.

And then he is gone and I am standing there like a stunned mullet, looking out at Em as she is nailing two pieces of wood together with Cass. For quite a while I just stand there not sure what to do, when to tell her that her sister is dead. Is there a right time?

I have crept out silently and I am sitting on a chair watching them, rocking back and forth, tears running silently down my cheeks. She looks up at me and instantly she knows something is very wrong. As she walks towards me she is saying,

"Tone, what's wr..." and then it hits her.

"What's happened, why did Totto need to call you?"

I look at her and hold my arms out to her. Instinctively she comes in to them and I am hugging her as I tell her. The first of the howls of pain leaves her gut. She pulls violently away from me, shaking her head, No... No... No ... No... No...!" howling, clenching her fists, her face contorted with grief...

***

And now I sit at my dog's grave, a grave I had dug a week ago, and I see me wrapping him up in my favourite coat and putting him to rest, a coat I was wearing when I picked him up from the pound 15 years before. The coat he slept on his last few years as he dragged his old body around following the sun.

Nine years have passed since I watched Em slide into an inescapable cave of grief. And now I hear her sobbing and saying,

"I just can't get over it. It's ruining everything, but I just can't get over it..."

Her sisters are crying now and trying to counsel her and I sit here listening to it all. And then it hits me. There is no way to fix it, it is a broken thing and it will always be broken. For nine years I had lived in the hope that she would come back, find some way to get through it. For our children's sake, for our sake, for her sake...

But it crippled her. And there was no going back.

Sledgehammer
40 years ago

      The Sampson's house is lit up all blue and red when we enter, the colours bouncing off the white walls and flooding the room. My brother and I are ushered into the lounge whilst my mother disappears down a hallway with my sleeping sister. We are told to sit down on the couch, one of those overstuffed 70's style vinyl couches that were everywhere at the time. I notice as I sit on the hard, slippery vinyl surface that it doesn't have any arms and the legs seem too small to carry its overstuffed load. I look up at Mr Sampson, who is standing there watching us. I feel insulated, like there is a thick wall between me and this experience. Sounds are distorted and my blurry eyes cannot seem to settle on anything, instead they dart about furtively. Mr Sampson is looking at us with a wry grin that unsettles me. My brother and I are both sitting forward, our backs straight and hands on our laps just like Mum had taught us to do when in someone else's house. Mr Sampson sees our forced look of comfort and says,

      "Sit back and relax, boys, it's nearly over now."

      I look at Mr Sampson's face. There's something self-satisfied about it. I hear my brother saying,

      "Thanks Mr Sampson."

I just stare at him. Their lounge room is large and has minimal furniture. Directly opposite us there is a huge TV dead centre of the wall and above it there are a few shelves and what looks like family photos hanging there. I stare at the happy faces looking back at me, the hair all perfect, standing there in their Sunday best with that vacant smile like they are waiting for the flash to go off and blind them. I squirm uncomfortably in my seat and the vinyl squeaks which for some reason makes me turn red with embarrassment, like I had farted and all that good training was shattered in an instant.

Mrs Sampson and her daughter Cheryl have entered the room and I crosscheck the reality against the eerie photos on the wall. Cheryl is saying something to her Dad, which I can't make out, except for the 'Oh Dad!' at the end as she puts her ten-year old hands on her hips and storms over to the TV and turns it on. Suddenly there is a blast of sound coming into the room and the black and white hues compete with the red and blue lights from outside for space on the walls.

"De… e...lllll Monti suits!" a voice cries into the room. Images of men in suits standing looking at the camera and shrugging their shoulders, checking the fit and looking confident, blasts onto our faces. The music swells as one of the men in suits winks to the camera, as if to say, 'c'mon ladies, I'm ready!'

"Look good…" drum roll.

"Feel good…" drum roll.

"Are good…" the announcer declares confidently, clasping his hands together for extra emphasis, with that same self-satisfied grin Mr Sampson is still wearing as he continues his staring at us. He is making me nervous now, so I turn away and look out the window at the street. I can see the police cars and the white car with the distraught woman, I can see the light bouncing off our broken stuff, I can see my father standing in front of the smashed lounge room window, a cop either side of him. They are talking to him, he has his head bowed and he is nodding from time to time.

I turn back around at Mr Sampson. He is looking right at me. I squirm again. Finally the smile retreats sideways off his face as he says,

"But maybe it'll never be over... for you..."

A Desert and a Slide Guitar
4 years ago

Harry has become 'Bazza' again and he is back on the bench seat, hunched over the wheel and peering straight ahead into the distant recesses of his rapidly eroding sanity. There is a lone amber light illuminating him in a tight, fuzzy pool of warmth when he talks and there is a cool blue with the same focus, tight and fuzzy, that fades up to replace the amber when the pre-recorded narration comes on.

The words are a rambling concoction of the delusional thoughts of a man feeling the cancer eating away at his soul, aware that his time is running out and the regrets are piling up like discarded second hand clothes around him. When the amber replaces the blue he becomes aware that he is driving through the vast cold desert night, dodging and cursing the roos that dance around in front of him and being blasted periodically by road train headlights, squinting at road signs that whizz past him, a blurry reminder that he is heading straight to nowhere.

And there isn't a chance in hell he can make a U-turn.

On Bazza's road there is only one direction available... straight at the stunned, blackened audience. I can feel their tension from the wings where I sit, staring out at the forestage through a gap in the curtains and listening to the mad, desperate ramblings of a man whose time had run out.

"Fuck! No wife, no kids, no brothers, or sisters, no house, nothing! Nothing to show for this life except a football ground full of empty stubbies, testimony to my ability to run away when anything gets close. Jesus, years went by and I didn't even notice. And where are my mythical fuckin' mates, hey? Either dead or entrenched in marriage and family or any other blight on the human spirit they could find. Fuckin' piss weak, I reckon, not a pair of balls between 'em all. Fuckin' better off without them..."

The light turns to blue and Bazza's voice over comes over the speakers.

"But Bazz, who's going to bury you? Must feel a little scary now, to have got to 65 and no-one will even notice when you are gone..."

Lights to amber, then Bazza says,

" Y...e...s they will... th... they'll pass 'round the hat at the pub..." but even he doesn't believe it.

Lights to blue and Bazza's voice-over.

"Think you've got it all worked out, don't ya? You think anyone gives a shit, Bazza? Muriel's the only one who might notice that you're gone mate, that's one! And you treated her like shit most of the time, didn't even make an honest woman of her and marry her! Need at least four pallbearers to carry you to the grave..."

Amber light.

"I ... don't like commitment, what can I say?"

Blue light.

"Gees mate, you seemed pretty committed to Carlton and United breweries!"

There is the familiar sound of a stubby being opened, a katishhsh sound, repeated over and over, and the clinking of stubbies as they land on each other, a hollow, glassy sound that makes Bazza's head drop and his tight grip loosen on the wheel.

Weakly, Bazza says, "Well why don't you just fuck off," adjusting the rear view mirror.

"Too late to look back Bazza, too late…"

I sit and watch, relieved to be bathed in darkness.

A shaft of light made by the curtain runs past my right foot and dissolves into the backstage darkness. I stand there immersed in Bazza's head state, watching the dimly illuminated faces of the front two rows of audience being carried away, transported into Bazza's twisted desperation. Stolen away for a moment from their ordinary lives in this ordinary city. Some have blankets over their knees due to the shit air-con that fails to evaporate the sweat pouring down Bazza's neck. The same air-con that makes the backstage area an icy, unfriendly space, this eerie buffer-zone between the artifice and reality.

And I was never quite sure which one was which…

I can hear Bazza whistling a familiar tune, an old tune. One I know intimately and yet the name escapes me. I am staring at the black curtain as if this will help me remember. It's an old jazz tune but I just can't get the title. And then I see my girls' faces, looking up at Jackson as he strums his old Macaferri guitar on my veranda many years ago. And then I've got it and I am humming along, staring out at the back of Bazza's head and the mesmerised audience. I can see Bazza's grip on the wheel tighten again for a second, then I watch as his shoulders slump back down again as he begins to sing the first verse.

'Grab your coat and get your hat
Leave your worries on the doorstep
Life can be so sweet
On the sunny side of the street... '

And after the first line he is sobbing, choking back tears as an unconvinced man sings a song that always used to pick him up, and this time it fails as he mumbles awkwardly,

"Sunny side of the street..."

The soft amber light fades slowly as he hangs his head against the wheel, crying with more gusto than we have seen of him, with more conviction than any of his pearls of wisdom could create. An eerie whistling of the tune comes over the speakers, fading in time with the light and Bazza is plunged into an even deeper darkness than before.

The audience is strangely silent, as if caught peering through a keyhole, they shuffle awkwardly in their seats, the whole room dark except for the 4 green exit signs on the doors to the foyer. I move aside as the other actors push the feral cat tree towards me, and the stage. I can sense the audience isn't sure if they should applaud or not and Bazza's continued crying isn't helping them decide, it being the only sound in the darkness and it has chilled us all to the bone. I turn and look over at Bek who is looking somewhat perturbed, this crying has gone on too long and she is waiting for Harry to come through into the wings so she can give the call for the next lighting state. The actors are waiting for him too, we are all waiting for Harry to climb out of the funk he is in, the very public funk.

Finally I hear movement on stage, the creaking of the springs of the bench seat and then the sluggish footsteps, one foot dragging behind the other. He is on his way. The actors breathe a collective sigh of relief and ready themselves for the push of the tree onto the stage. Harry walks past me, inches away but he does not see me. But I see his tortured face as it glides past, almost floating, illuminated by the next lighting state that Bek has finally been able to call, a dark blue state. I watch Harry sit over in the corner near the props table, clasping his hands and rocking back and forth slightly as the actors wheel the tree onto stage in bright, full light and Ry Cooders 'Paris Texas' fades up to cover their moves and fades down again as the actors make their exits, each one peeling off behind a different curtain and disappearing again into the darkness...

The Raffle
20 years ago

Time, in a hospital, moves like an old whore with a smack habit. Every day blurs into the one before and the one before that and then it becomes just one long fucking day, the same day. Since I had been here my time came in 4 hour bursts thanks to the morphine, but now it had no end, every day dragged itself around scowling and tripping over its IV trolley and getting caught in curtains. It was the grim realist version of the Bold and the Beautiful without the meaningful look off-camera after a difficult emotional moment, without the ridiculously handsome saving lives and bedding the nurses AND the emotional wife of the patient whilst ignoring calls from his 4th wife who's ringing to say she's dropping in to see him. No exotic dramas here, just the stink of disinfectant and the howls of people in pain. Just the stunned look of a young girl as she grapples with the aftermath of being scalped by a grain harvester, her long hair having dragged her into the shredder. Everywhere, the stench of pain of people who had been plucked out of their lives and changed forever. Got a feeling we wouldn't get a daytime slot for this fucking circus.

I am out on the 7th floor balcony smoking a cigarette and looking out towards the city. It is hot already and it's still early, the brown sludge air not spreading across the whole metropolis yet. There seems to be some sort of big traffic jam, people are out of their cars and peering ahead of them, horns are blaring, an ambulance struggles to make progress even with sirens and lights flashing and as I look closer I can see the problem. The ambulance was using the tram-lines in the middle of the road but they seem to be full of trams. I can see hundreds of trams all butting up to each other, a long line of them heading down Elizabeth Street. And they are going nowhere. Down at the massive roundabout I see the flash of someone welding, kneeling over the tracks. *What is he doing?* I ponder. There seems to be a crowd gathered, watching, most of them in high visibility vests and holding placards. And then I remember hearing two nurses talking about how long it took them to get to work because of the 'bloody tram strike' and realise that the man is welding the tracks together so that they can't move the long line of trams trailing down Elizabeth Street, right through the middle of the city, to Flinders Street station.

It has been eight weeks since I have read a paper or turned on a TV, but this industrial unrest had been going on for months, long before I turned down that dirt road a lifetime ago.

They, the government that is, were trying to get rid of Melbourne's famous tram conductors and replace them with ticket machines because people weren't 'economically viable' anymore. There had been a couple of minor strikes but this one was for real and the 'trammies' had had enough of fearing for their jobs and had crippled the tram system and blocked a third of the traffic that funnelled into the city... Trammies were part of the fabric of the place, what the fuck was the government thinking? All sorts of people became trammies, from all walks of life. Part of the fun of a tram ride was in not knowing what sort of trammie you would get. Sometimes you would get an oldie who'd been riding the trams for 50 years and called everyone 'love' and made sure sullen teenagers gave their seat to an old person. You could get an Indian with very little English, you could get a footy fanatic who would sing his club's theme song whilst giving out tickets and maybe he might snarl if someone got on wearing another team's colours. You could get a juggler who tried to brighten the days of the drones as they made another instalment on their slow death. Sometimes an acting student, or better still an out of work actor trying to make ends meet and practicing their craft on their moving electric stage.

It was a great feeling to be in a tram full of people laughing and just letting go of that tightness around the shoulders for a little while. And the government was taking it away because it was un-fucking-economic, gripped as they were, and still are, by the cultural suffocation of 'economic rationalism', as if all that mattered was some good looking numbers on a piece of paper.

"Aah there you are Mr Cameron!"

I turned quickly and instinctively put out my cigarette with my right slipper.

"Oh oh, Mum's caught me smoking again!", continuing to look out at the strike action.

It is one of the nurses and I turn just in time to see her mocking frown turn to a smile.

"What's up, nurse?" I turn back to the city traffic mess, pointing with my good arm, "Trammie's strike, yeah?"

"Yeah," she replies, "makes it hard to get to work on time, the roads are jammed, the trains are groaning under the extra load, everyone's kind of angry cause they're late… it's hot… you know, another day in 'Marvellous Melbourne'," she says, inverting the last two words with her fingers, a reference to an old tourism slogan. "Now, I've come to get you 'cause it's time to put on your skin grafts! And guess what? I get to do them!"

"So happy for you," pausing as I look at her name badge, "Tina."

As she removes the bandages and starts to gently pull the waxy dressing off my raw flesh I try to remember the last time I saw it exposed. Was it two weeks? Two days? A month?

The shock of seeing half my arm without any skin makes my body shudder and a hypersensitive shiver attacks my raw flesh. I take in air through gritted teeth.

"You OK?"

"Um... yep. Just a shock to see it – that's all. It's been a while."

"Well it's gonna look pretty different soon, that's for sure," looking across at the sealed containers that, I guess, have the harvested skin from my thighs in them. She is laying out a drop sheet under my arm, which she lifts gently and miraculously the pain is minimal, just the oversensitive skin and a dull bone ache, which seems metres below my exposed flesh. Now she is opening one of the containers and peering inside and I peer in as well. My skin is lying in some sort of liquid and has crumpled itself up at the edges so it resembles an old, discarded lemon peel. It looks much smaller than the area it has to cover and I wonder if there will be enough to do the job. She picks up the skin with two tweezers and gently pulls at it and I watch as it expands to 4 times its size. She moves the skin over the top of my arm, looks at me and says,

"OK, lets do this thing!"

She places it down on the flesh and I tense up, expecting a burst of pain, but there is nothing except a slightly cool and slimy feeling. I watch as she spreads it over my arm, sliding it around until she is happy with the position. Then she grabs one edge of the skin and pulls it and when she gets to the edge of the wound, places it down and says,

"Watch this, it's really cool."

The skin seems to suck onto the flesh like there is some kind of adhesive involved... She pats it down gently and every time she pats it down I feel it 'grab' onto my flesh, like it is already growing on it.

She gets out the next piece and lays it next to the other one and once again I watch as she pats it down and it sucks onto my flesh. When she has covered all the flesh she trims the excess skin off like a really messed up dressmaker, then puts the scissors back on the trolley and leans back to take in her handy work.

"God, I love doing skin grafts! "

"God, I am glad that you do," I reply, starting to enjoy her energy.

"OK, let's do the stomach then! "

**

After she has finished and left I stare out the window, this one having a broken view of Royal parade. I can see the yellow and green line of trams and it looks like more are being added to the line. I can feel the tension coming off the street as the traffic jam strangles the city flow. I try to move my fingers, I try to make a fist but fail, and I wonder how long before I can get out of here and get back to my family, get back to my life.

And then the realisation hits me that there is no going back to anything, that my life as I knew it had ceased to exist and there is nothing I can do about it...

Liquid Moments
6 months ago

I am watching the last mix of the day spinning around in the concrete mixer and finally I have got one right. The mix folds over itself like a wave and I become hypnotised as I lean against the handle, feeling each roll of weight under my hand. It's been a long haul, this paving gig, and I am keen for it to be over, it being the last big job left to do on the house. I have been working on back-to-back shows and paving in any time period that turned up. I was even doing a couple of quick mixes of a morning before an afternoon start on a show, turning most days into an 18 hour proposition that miraculously never seemed to leave me feeling drained. My body clock is all over the place due to the odd and ever changing show schedule and yet I still get out of bed after a few hours sleep ready to do it all over again.

I was driven by the desire to get out from under the weight of a mortgage so big I would never pay it off in a lifetime, out of a job so demanding of my time that it left little else except recovery time. And I wasn't getting much of that, nor did I seem to need it.

I look up from the mesmerising mixer and take in the vista around me. The 20 year long drought had broken a couple of months ago and the place looks amazing. Rolling, green hills, the sound of the swollen river rushing down to Cairn Curran reservoir, my twisted steel and wood sculptures spread out over the green, freshly mown grass, the trees bursting with the light green leaves of new growth. The hundreds of shrubs I had planted over the years that I thought had died have burst forth with new, abundant growth. Some of the wattles are flowering as they emerge from their long, dry sleep. The land has breathed a collective sigh of relief. Birds are in abundance and flying busily from tree to shrub to gnarly sculpture, to the soft, brown earth where a smorgasboard of worms and insects awaits them.

Ben Harper is throbbing over the top of the cacophony of birds, a soulful blues number 'I Want to be Ready', one of my favourites, and I zoom in on that, the whir and clang of the mixer fading down with the birds...

> *'How I am strong*
> *Is to know what makes me weak.*
> *How I am found*
> *Is to know just whom I seek...'*

I place the wheelbarrow underneath the mixer and pull the handle towards me and watch the mix slide gently into the barrow in one fluid movement, and I steady the load with my knee as the lump of concrete settles in. Ben is singing,

> *'I want to be reeeaady*
> *I want to be reyeyeady*
> *I want to be reaaaaaddddy*
> *Ready to put on my long white robe,'*

as I put my hands on the wheelbarrow, bend my knees and walk off towards the back of the house and the beautiful random pieces of slate waiting patiently in little piles. I walk the barrow over last weeks paving and land it on the edge. As it slides to a stop I have the shovel in my hands and I count each full shovel as I hurl them onto the crushed rock bed the pavers will sit on. After ten I stop and get the trowel and start distributing the concrete evenly whilst eyeing off the piles, looking for the first one that will go down.

After 180 square metres of paving I have become adept at finding the right paver quickly, almost instinctively, and before long I am cleaning an arrow shaped paver with a stiff brush and placing it gently on top of the concrete bed. Then the next and the next appear, all different shapes, and are being placed around the arrow paver. Within 15 minutes I have a square metre laid out and ready to be bedded down. I use the end of the handle of the trowel and my left hand to work them down to the right height, then a straight edge over all of them until I can hear the straight- edge touching the previously laid pavers and I know it is done. I don't even do the usual double or triple check for height discrepancies, instead I grab the shovel and put the other half of the mix onto the last unpaved rock bed. Half an hour later I am patting down the last slate paver and it is then I stop to look at the job. I think about the irony of finally getting good at something at the end of the job, I think about all the time I had spent fucking around getting one rock pretty close to perfect and plopping the next one down which would then mess with the first one. *Jesus, how many hours had I spent doing that before I got it?*

I think of the intense realisation of finishing a house too late, after everyone has gone, like some pointless gesture. But something had kicked in years ago, a strange determination, the will to not be like my father, the chance to show my girls that you can do anything you focus your mind on, be good at anything you choose and it was your attitude to yourself that revealed itself along the way, that even handicaps can be embraced and overcome if you choose to experience that. I think of the years immediately after the accident and how I huddled under the warm blanket of hopelessness, how I let my mangled arm become a reason not to be able to do something. It all seemed so long ago now.

The light is fading from the sky as I clean the concrete mixer, throwing round rocks in with the water to knock off any resistant lumps of concrete stuck to the walls. I watch the birds do their last bit of foraging, I look around, 15 years since I drove the first peg into the ground, and realise it is done now, finished, ready for sale. Probably 5 years too late, but it was done.

The Audreys' song '*Small Things*' is playing when I walk into the house, as if on cue. I pour a large whisky into a small glass and gulp it down whilst leaning against the new terrazzo kitchen benches, listening.

> *'And there's one thing that I'm keeping*
> *Out of all the things I've found*
> *Is that the best way to be heard sometimes*
> *Is not to make a sound...'*

I pour another drink and stare out at my beautiful home as the song plays loudly, filling every nook and cranny.

> *'And all it takes to find your feet*
> *Is just to stand your ground...'*

I drink to that and marvel at the intense irony of having no one to share this moment with, and maybe it was better this way. No sledgehammer can smash this place down, I have made sure of that. I pour another drink and as I do the gnawing feeling of hunger leaves me. It seems that gulping whisky on an empty stomach is the call for the evening. I embrace this thought by adding ice and coke to the equation. And then it comes to me, what I have been doing all these years, after my children moved out, years after the family dissolved.

I am sweeping the stage after the show, I am a lonely figure in an expanse of blackness, the empty auditorium an eerie witness to the somewhat futile gesture.

I gulp down the rest of my drink and pour another, the song reaching its climax.

> *'And fallin's not that hard when you're starting*
> *out so low*
> *And drowning's not that bad*
> *If you breathe*
> *And just let go...'*

I am swaying with the whisky when the tears come, but there is something making me smile as well. I feel the liquidity of the moment, I see myself dissolving into the walls as I finish the render with a wet brush, I see myself rolling over and over on the floor with my girls after the new carpet was laid and we relished the soft feeling for the first time, our laughter echoing through the empty house.

I walk into the lounge room and sit down next to the man with the 'outstretched hand' piece of wood I found with Kath and Noi four years ago. I look at it, as I have been doing most nights, taking in every detail, every twist and turn in the petrified wood. I have cleaned it and mounted it on a twisted steel stand, which has it sitting around waist height now. And during the last few months I have been sanding, cleaning, admiring this moment of generosity petrified by time, the hands outstretched offering itself up in an eternal moment of hope.

I slump down next to it, curl into a ball and sleep.

A Beach in Thailand
Present

The largest set of the day is forming in the distance. I can see the shadow created by the crest of the wave and I can feel the silent menace through the sand as it approaches. The log seems oblivious to the impending disaster and has somehow maintained a rough position ever since I slumped down and dropped my stash of treasures what now seems like days ago. I am a trembling mess and I feel like I am on the edge of something, something big. Some shift has occurred in me, and I realise that I have been running away from this for 40 years, conveniently hiding in the bush, or huddling down behind the set whilst the show goes on beyond the wall. Every chance I have had I have looked the other way; have gone looking for the shiny thing to distract my attention, and the life I have stumbled through is a glaring testimony to this. How many times have I put my faith in another and been fucked over, how many chances does one get?

Phee Noi and Phee Nan are walking along the beach as the tide recedes, leaving piles of wood, huge logs and heaps of plastic for them to pick through and I smile in their direction, sensing their collective joy. They are somehow in their element picking through the discarded, rolling over the lost, turning over wood battered smooth on this last leg of a long journey, possible years of swirling around the coasts of Indonesia, Thailand, Burma and India.

The set comes in and the first wave crashes onto the beach with a thunderous fury that makes the ground shudder under me. I see Phee Noi and Phee Nan look up out at the ocean and then make a brisk retreat further up the beach away from the back crushing power of the surf. I seem unable to move and brace myself as the white-water rushes up the beach towards me, enveloping me. I hold my sitting position in the 2 feet of foamy water and watch as my stash of wood is sucked back into the ocean. If the ocean wants me today, thinking of a Tom Waits song, then it can have me...

The next wave is even bigger, a 10 foot high wall of brooding anger approaching the beach. I brace myself and then, just as the wave delivers itself with pure intention onto the beach, I let go. I let myself go just like my log and let it just hit me and this time it picks me up like I am weightless and hurls me, tumbling, further up the beach just like another piece of junk. The ocean seems to be cleansing itself, it is spitting out the inedible and the toxic, trying with all its might to expel the refuge of humanity that has reached dangerously toxic levels.

The wave recedes and leaves me face down in the sand. I lie still for a moment, then raise my head and shake some of the sand off my face. My chest is heaving as I struggle to suck air in without coughing. I sense the next wave coming and this time I start rolling over and over, my arms pinned to my sides, away from the wave. When the white water wall hits me I am already moving, rolling over, being tossed around and around. I am holding my breath, which is running low, when I am slammed into something big and immobile, knocking the wind out of me. It takes me a moment to realise I have just been slammed into the sandbank as the wave starts to recede, leaving me embedded in the wall.

I roll off laughing and wheezing, holding my gut in like it wants to escape. I roll back down the ever-steepening beach towards the next freak wave, which is about to break and I stop to watch. As it peaks, the wind seems to pick it up, somehow giving it another 5 feet of wall and hollows it out into a cylinder of destruction. I start rolling away from it when I hear it crashing onto the sand, and this time I curl up into a tight ball, the white water swirls around me and then I am rolling over and over again. A Michael Leunig poem comes into my head as I am carried with great speed towards the sand wall again.

> *'Let it go*
> *Let it out*
> *Let it all unravel... '*

Suddenly I collide with what feels like a log and a momentary fear takes over me as I hope that the ocean has had time to soften or break all the jagged branches off it. Time slides away from me, *why haven't I hit the wall yet?* Even though I am rolling fast it seems to be in slow-mo, the faster I am rolled, the slower it gets until the wave is finished with me and I lie splayed flat on my back on the beach, laughing, surrounded by plastic and wood and rope and nets, flip flops, cigarettes lighters and lost toys.

> *'Let it free*
> *And it can be*
> *A path on which to travel'*

My legs and back bear the brunt of it, and then we are rolling together. I stare up at the sky as another plane roars above my head, and I watch as it turns from silver to pink to amber in the morning light and disappears into a low, dark cloud, emerging finally, banks right and heads north, to the madness of Bangkok and beyond.

The Raffle
20 years ago

I had begun walking around the entire hospital, through all the wards, into the cafeteria where I would watch normal, healthy people eating normal, healthy food. I had lost 10 kilograms and my skinny, wasted legs struggled to carry me around, but with each day they got stronger. Often I would sit in the emergency ward of a night time and listen to all the people with their various wounds and maladies, half of them drunk or wasted on drugs, bemoaning the incredibly slow service. I would watch exhausted nurses struggle under the emotional load of dealing with so many people in pain, out of whack, disempowered, lost. The wails of pain would echo up the corridors and cling to the walls. The busy scuffs of the nurse's shoes joined the pain, creating an arresting rhythm of distress.

Friday and Saturday nights were the busiest of all as one ambulance after another would scream into the emergency ward entrance with sirens blaring, delivering yet another drunk driver to his possible salvation, wheeling another fanatical drunk football supporter into the ward who had unleashed himself on an unwary social drinker in a pub somewhere, anywhere, all over the city. These were the nights the pressure valve was released and I struggled to imagine how it could be any other way, as a lifetime of slow disempowerment will eventually make people blow. Without football there would be chaos within weeks. I would sit out the front and watch the ambulance drivers hosing the blood out of their ambulances, the colour drained from their faces, an expression of defeated disbelief, stuck with the realisation that their job consisted of saving the stupid and irresponsible and cleaning up the messes they created of others.

Often I would end up in parts of the hospital I wasn't meant to be in and there were times when I had to muster all my charm to be allowed to continue, laying a trail of half truths which I would follow in a jagged fashion back to my ward, where there was a bed waiting, a sagging Christmas tree and my mate, Peter.

I had become addicted to pain and now mine was largely gone, I searched it out in others. A whole lot of bullshit was peeled off people when they were strapped to a bed and screaming at the place their leg used to be. The feeling that there was no time anymore, just the intensity of the now, seemed to liberate feelings out from under the normal social etiquette, out from under the crushing banality. It was like hanging out with a hundred people with Asperger's. Here we all were, with the stench of disinfectant and rotting flesh, whilst all around us the city boiled up like the biggest festering wound of all...

One evening, I found myself in the burns unit, being drawn there by the sound of a man laughing hysterically. Intrigued by this incongruous sound I wandered down the corridor past many rooms full of bandaged, immobile, raw human beings until eventually I was there, standing in the doorway beyond which the laughter lay, the sound buoyant and with a rawness all its own.

I swayed a little and leaned my left shoulder against the door jam and tilted my head to the sound of his laughter like a dog would to a high-pitched squeal. He was telling a joke to the nurses, a dirty joke that sat on a bed of socially accepted misogynism, and he didn't give a fuck that the nurses were female. He delivered the punch line and launched into some more wild laughter that you can't help but join in on. Even the nurses couldn't resist.

The man was clearly insane and I wanted to meet him…

He was lying in some kind of harness that suspended him just above the bed and as he laughed the whole thing shook, sending ripples of the sound of clanging metal out into the room. One of his arms was missing, leaving a bandaged stump just below the shoulder in its place. His feet were also heavily bandaged, in fact, both of his legs were. He had dark, dirty, medium length hair and a bushy, dark beard that seemed to stick to his face like an unwanted guest: someone who had stumbled into the wrong funeral and was trying to back out of the room again. But this guy's smile held it there against its will. I shuffled up to him, smiling.

He looked over the top of a couple of giggling nurses and yelled,

"GIIIDAY MATE! I'm Ben, what's your name?"

"Tony," I replied.

"Well Tone, I'm glad you're here. I mean, for fuck's sake, I'm wearing out my audience," looking at the nurses and winking at them suggestively.

"It's alright girls, you go ahead with your job, don't mind me and Tone, we'll just have a chat whilst you scrape more dead flesh off me, okey doke?"

There were two large lumps on the underside of his thighs all bandaged up, and one of the nurses began unwrapping one as Ben looked deliriously at her and said,

"Boy, if I wasn't strapped down here…"

He looked across at me and winked, halving the intense pools of blue boring into me, giving me a moments respite from the insane clarity that lay there.

"Well, don't be shy, Tone, come on over and enjoy the show!"

I walked around to the other side of the bed. He didn't take his eyes off me as I did, and he began whistling happily. When I got to him I raised my left hand and grab his brother-style, and gave him a semi-decent squeeze, which he returned immediately, widening his grin and saying,

"How the fuck are ya?"

"Alright mate," I heard myself replying, "been through the worst of it for me and I am spat out the other end wandering around in a daze. What in the hell happened to you, mate?"

He grimaced for a moment as the bandage the nurse was taking off got stuck on something, and then quickly the smile returned with the desperateness of an exhausted rock climber looking for a solid footing and staring down at the abyss below him.

"Oh, you know Tone, the usual kind of thing. Got on the piss with me mates after work, then decided to break into an electricity substation and get myself blown to bits! As far as a nights go, it was pretty memorable I s'pose…"

His understatement was so thick and abundant it settled into a pool below his bed, and for the nurses it was just another mess to be cleaned up.

They had removed the dressing now and I peered over the bed to get a close look. There appeared to be a soft lump of skin and flesh sown onto it, a large, fatty looking lump.

"Yeah, blew me feet off, blew me arm off and blew a hole in me side. Nurse? Can you lift up my gown up and show Tone the shotgun blast?"

She nodded and gently pulled his gown up, revealing what was left of his body.

"Oh yeah, blew me dick off as well! That was the funniest part, 'cept no one seems to get the joke Tone!"

I looked at the bandaged remains of his genitals and then saw the gaping chunk that was missing from his stomach and back. It did look like a shotgun blast. There were also long, straight lines of bruises running up and down his chest and legs. He saw me looking, my smile had gone and there was a jagged lump in my throat instead.

"Don't lose the plot on me yet, mate, I haven't got to the best part, the *piece de resistance* if you will, the crowning glory, the fuckin' bees knees..."

He started whistling again, a random melody with no end, a cheery substitute for the tears of despair that threatened to overcome him at any moment, the hysterical, blunt truth that his stupidity had completely fucked his life. *Or maybe that was just me projecting my shit onto him, maybe he was the happiest he had ever been, how was I to know?* And then I realised that it didn't matter at all anyway, nothing fucking mattered.

My grin returned as his whistle became a chortle, then a snicker, then more snickers and then he was laughing again and I was too. We were laughing like we had just watched a Monty Python movie whilst stoned. It was the best virus in the hospital and you couldn't help but catch it. Soon the nurses were laughing too, surrendering their scraping tools to the moment, the laughter building until tears of pure joy were welling up in us all. Except for Ben. His eyes were dry as a bone, his expression exactly the same as De Niro's mad smile from Taxi Driver. Eventually the laughter subsided, the nurses picked up their tools and continued cleaning the lumpy mounds on his thighs.

"So, the ultimate hilarity is yet to come, my new friend, and I am sure you will find it a side-splitting detail."

Looking at him, "Well how much worse can it get? There's only half of you left!"

"Aah, that's the spirit Tone, take the piss. I can't get enough of that around here, they're all so fucking uptight, like they're dealing with life and death or something! Yeah, so here it is... Tone, they are moving my arse cheeks down my legs slowly and are going to cover the deep fried stumps that used to be my feet... I will literally be standing on my arse if I am lucky. And Tone, that's one thing I am, is lucky!"

I looked at the lumps that were his arse cheeks stitched on to his thighs as the nurse dabbed away at the clear ooze coming out of them.

"Yeah, they walk 'em down my legs like an overfed caterpillar and for a couple of weeks it stays there as the blood supply adjusts, then they walk 'em down some more... fucking hilarious I reckon, it's like a horse race that takes 8 to 10 weeks for the arse cheeks to cross the finish line. We are all taking bets on whether 'Lefty' or ' Mr Right' will make it first... fucking hilarious!"

I looked into his mad blue eyes. It was the only way for him now, this insane humour. I tried not to check to see whether 'Lefty' was winning or not.

"So what makes you so lucky Ben, it kinda looks like your life's fucked now..."

"Whoa, harsh Tone! I am the luckiest person alive because I was wearing runners." He paused whilst I pondered what that meant, then I understood, so he continued,

"'Cause if I wasn't, I would've been earthed to the ground and that would've meant instant death for me cause the electricity would've stayed in my body until I was fully fried, rather than blast out in random and yet gruesomely artistic ways..."

He laughed again.

"And I wouldn't have got this blinding reality to laugh my way through, I wouldn't get to stare down this nurse's dress and wonder what her breasts look like, I wouldn't have got to smell the burning flesh as I lay there on the ground afterwards wondering what the fuck happened, I wouldn't get to feel so fucking alive I feel like I'm goin' to burst. If I was religious I would say I have been reborn. I have been given a second chance and no matter what I will never stop laughing, Tone, ever. I am the luckiest man alive because now I really get to live. I have been woken up, Tone, and it feels fucking great!"

There was silence between us. Ben cleared his throat, which was dry and raspy from all the raving.

"And what about you, Tone, are you alive, really fuckin' alive?"

His eyes shone like a man possessed.

A Desert and a Slide Guitar
4 years ago

Bazza sits very upright on the bench seat, his
eyes wide open, he looks stunned and lost. He holds
the wheel with his arms locked straight and he is
swaying ever so slightly. I am unsure whether it is the
rocking of the 'car' or the pulsating rhythm of Bazza's
racing heartbeat that is producing the sway. He
seems unaware of the random headlights that bath
him sporadically in a clear, white light. The white
light is small and dim at the start and is coming from
above and in front of him, building in intensity as
more lights fade up and join the first two in the slow
build to full. As the 'truck' passes lights on the front
edge of the stage floor go on and throw Bazza's
shadow onto the set behind him, the enlarged
shadow of his head landing on the feral cat tree. The
sound of the truck is muffled compared to other
times, and there is no back projection to give it a
sense of reality. A lot of reverb has been added,
rendering the truck's sound weak and somehow
ineffectual, a surreal shadow of its former self. Bazza
sits through the barrage of lights completely unfazed,
his stare a fixed burning thing, like an ant frying
under a magnifying glass.

Harry has applied a deathly looking make-up
to Bazza's face. His eyes are sunken with dark rings
around them set against a grey/ white foundation
make-up. The only definition is the black painted

lines of his forehead. He looks dead already from where I stand on the opposite side of stage, in the wings. His white make-up finishes crudely on his jawline and I can see Bazza gulping, his large adam's apple travelling up and down his throat like a pole dancer whose power has left her. Just past Bazza's hands and the steering wheel I can see the green EXIT sign above the foyer door and I marvel at the poignant angle only I can see. If only Bazza could see that sign. *There are exits everywhere, but which one?*

Bazza's head starts to droop and then he snaps back awake, eyes wide with shock. His eyes close slowly again and as his head slumps down with them, a truck's horn can be heard rising up in the distance. Bazza wakes up again with a start, his eyes blinking in a vain attempt to kick-start his mind but he seems to fail. He slumps over the wheel, making it skew to the left. His head is sliding down off the wheel towards the seat when again he wakes and sits up, the dolly swerving wildly from side to side as the sound of a car sliding in dirt comes over the speakers.

"Holy fuck!" Bazza exclaims, which makes the audience laugh nervously.

Bazza is now careering around in circles and every time he is facing the audience he turns the wheel violently from side to side and his head lurches along behind the moves. Suddenly he pushes the dolly backwards and then across the forestage, sliding to a stop at the edge of the lit area, then back again to centre stage whereupon he flings the dolly backwards upstage and finally comes to a stop.

"I've gotta get off this road. So tired now, so tired… just … wanna… lie… down."

Bazza takes the next 'turn' left and he is bouncing up and down in his seat, echoing the corrugations in the road. He pushes the dolly around a few corners and then comes to a stop in front of the tree, his back to the audience.

"What the faarrrk?" he shouts, looking up at the tree.

His 'headlights' illuminate the tree momentarily and then he cuts the motor, the lights dimming over a couple of seconds until he is plunged into a dim, low amber light, as if a weak moon is shining half heartedly from a distance.

I am standing a few metres from Bazza, in the wings. He still has his back to the audience and he stares up at the feral cat tree. He has the face of a small boy looking at the dodgem cars at the circus. He gets out of the car but he is lost in his hypnotic stare as he kicks the dolly out of the way, over towards me. I put a foot out and stop it before it whacks me in the shin, thankful for not having to stifle a scream of pain. Bazza tilts his head ever so slightly and winks at me. *Bastard knew I was there! But how? He was all the way down stage when I crept quietly to where I am now.*

Bazza walks around the tree, looks at all the feral cat paper lanterns hanging off all the branches with a look of a man who has just found some kind of God. He doesn't look sleepy at all. The tree is bathed in the soft amber moon lighting, its branches devoid of leaves, of any signs of growth. It is a stout tree under lights, with a thick, twisted trunk and deformed looking branches and it reminds me of my beloved 'mistletoe' mutations at home.

This tree, however, was painted Styrofoam over a steel skeletal frame and right then I could imagine the set designer carving away at the Styrofoam with a grinder, watching his vision come alive in front of him behind a mask and safety glasses, way before Bazza would be walking around it on stages all over the country. Way before I would be standing metres away from it, in the darkness of the backstage moment...

Sledgehammer
40 years ago

I wasn't sure what Mr Sampson was talking about but I did know that I didn't like or trust him. Something about the beady eyes and the self-satisfied expression made me nervous. And I was already freaked out and yet, a strange calm had settled over me. I felt like if a bomb went off in this room right now I would merely have to brush the dust off my body and stroll out onto the street whilst the others would be blown apart, blown to pieces, blown into non existence, blown into the next horrific childhood moment. *What was wrong with me? Why couldn't I feel this moment like everyone else?*

The scene also felt strangely familiar, like I had been here before, like all the others were actors playing their parts to an audience after many weeks of rehearsals. Some of the household items had settled at the feet of the neighbours, who were peering up at the wrecked house that was my home. Collected together like the rubbish in the gutters, to be picked through by vagrants before making their way, like everything else, into the creeks and rivers and finally into the ocean, the rubbish dump of the human experience...

My brother is sobbing quietly and staring at the TV, biting his nails down to the quick. When I look at him I start sobbing too, my tears breaking the banks of the wall I had built for them, the wall that my father had built with that one look, that one comment. I wasn't scared anymore, I was terrified. Terrified and numb, everything felt like a dream. The TV seemed the only dull constancy around me so I pulled my attention from the bewildered sadness of my brother's face to the TV show that was blasting his face with shadows.

It was an American cop show called 'Adam 12'. The title was running over a bird's eye view shot of a police car with a large '12' painted on the roof driving down an L.A road, weaving around cars, lights flashing and a horn section dominating the music with their dramatic melody. Then it cut to a medium shot of the two cops in the car, and we are looking at them as if we are perched on their bonnet. Their names appear in gold letters at the bottom of the frame and one of them, the blond haired one, lifts one corner of his mouth into a grin, an 'it's gonna be alright now, we are here, we are cops' grin and I can't help but drag my attention to Mr Sampson's grin which is still plastered all over his face. He is now sitting in his Jason Recliner Rocker. *What was it with men's grins? Do they all do that? Look kind of smug and confident and kind of mad?* I tried to make my face do the same, why not? It was all around me, smug and confident men. My grin came out different, more of a pained, weeping bravado. *Maybe it would take years to perfect this skill,* I thought.

The cops on the TV are knocking on the door of a house as the cops on my street are walking my father out of my house and down towards the waiting police cars. The woman in the white car has climbed out and is waiting for my father. She is looking across at the house as the main cop is talking to her. My father has his hands behind his back and has a cop either side of him, holding an arm each, locking their hands around his elbows, making it appear they were out for a stroll on a sunny Sunday afternoon instead of arresting an ordinary man trapped in a rage that was destroying him and anything within his reach.

The cops on the TV are talking to a long haired bearded guy whose eyes are darting all about the place, holding the door ajar, just enough for them to see him. One of the cops frowns at the other like 'this is bullshit', then the other one launches himself at the hippy and they both fall into the room on top of each other and a scuffle ensues, flanked by the other cop who has drawn his weapon and is shouting,

"OK, OK break it up!"

The cops on the TV arrest the man, cuff him and lead him out the door as the cops on my street surround my father at the police cars, the main cop's face inches from my father's. The mad grin leaves my father's face as the cop slams him in the stomach, doubling him over…

The cops on the TV are walking down the front steps of the house when the hippy makes a run for it, darting off to the right with his arms behind his back and I see him crouch down and break into a sprint, just like my brother does on the footy field. The blonde cop throws down his police hat and makes chase. The camera pans away from the house and follows the action just in time to see the blonde cop tackle the hippy and bring him down. There is a clunky cut to a close-up of the blonde cop with his knee in the back of the hippy, saying,

"You have the right to remain silent…" as the cops out on my street are taking turns slamming my father in the guts, two of them holding him up so he doesn't collapse onto the ground and crawl to safety underneath the cop cars, which I am sure he would if he could…

The cops on the TV rough-handle the hippy into the back of their car and hop in the front, a cage between them and the hippy, who doesn't look dangerous or violent... The cops out on my street are trying to disperse the neighbours, I can see the main cop's chest heaving from the workout on my father's gut as he points with his finger and gestures for them to go. The Thompsons, in their pyjamas and slippers, nod their heads, turn around and walk off. The Rowes look reticent about going back inside, their little girl Nina's eyes are wide with excitement and she is resisting as her Mum takes her hand and pulls her towards their house.

The cops on the TV are driving along now and the blonde one is talking into the police radio, saying,

"This is Adam 12. We have the suspect in custody, our ETA is 15 minutes."

"Roger that Adam 12," a female voice replies.

The cops on my street have bundled my father and the woman in the white car into one of the police cars and are turning around to leave when my mother comes into the room, sits down between my brother and I. She is crying and holding us tightly to her as she looks out at the police cars leaving.

"It'll be alright, believe me, it'll be alright," she sobs.

I look out on the street. I look at the TV. Then I look out onto the street again and watch the cars taking my father away and I hope I will never see him again. I look at the TV as the music swells and the camera zooms out above the police car. Another job done, another day fighting the good fight, keeping America free and righteous. I look out at my street as the blue and red lights fade and the streetlights take over again, the flickering yellow that I remember, before all this started.

I stare again at the TV as an ad comes on for 'PATRA – Patra orange juice, the only one with the real orange taste.'

My mother has released us from her crushing hug and is wiping her eyes and blowing her nose.

What was real? One thing I knew for sure, the orange juice wasn't...

A Beach in Thailand
Present

I think I have seen those blue/ red flashing lights every day of my life, punctuating my dreams with their ominous intent, pushing their way through the crowded streets of my thoughts. I sit here on this beach, waves tossing me around like a piece of driftwood and I can see them now. I can see my father's sick grin hanging over the swell as it pounds the beach continuously. I see my stunned immobility, I see the fire that has burned in me since that day 40 years ago. I see the slow understanding that nothing is real at all and that I have hidden in the illusion, the construct, the art that imitates life, like a drunk uncle playing charades in front of a Christmas tree somewhere, some time.

It is in the time that never ends, it is in the sweat pouring down the side of the face of the tortured actor, forever drifting between the two worlds. It's in the ruptured grasp with which I hold onto reality. It's in the playfulness of knowing that the foundations of truth are eroded, being smashed constantly by the waves until it is hard to see if they are there at all. It's in the eyes of a small boy listening to the kindergarten teacher talking about the human skeleton underneath our skin and asking her to prove it. It's in the sideways baulk on the football ground as another opponent twice my size tries to tackle me and me somehow knowing which way to go. It was my hand going out instinctively to catch the balls my brother would throw at me, and me at him, throughout my childhood, the balls that eventually looked the size of watermelons. It was in seeing the move before it happened. It was in the watching of a moment like I wasn't really in it at all.

And for those few times that I saw the magic, there have been thousands of others I have not seen. I have blundered through my life like a drunk gambler hitting Vegas. And I have washed up on this beach, all my sharp edges blunted by life, worn smooth by the few moments of true bliss I have felt. I am a fucking fool, now I am reduced to my bare essence, the ocean washing the layers off me slowly as I roll over and over, the sea lice riddling what is left of me with holes. I am a fucking idiot, a blithering, sobbing mess at 44 years old... *how the fuck did it end up like this?*

There is no-one sitting next to me. I am alone, comprehensively alone. Phee Noi and Phee Nan might as well be 100 kilometres away from me given the place I have gone to.

A surge of warmth rises up inside of me, starting in my gut and flooding my being. As each wave slides up the beach and cascades around me, I just let it in. Let it become a part of me until I can't work out where I stop and the ocean begins. The log I have been watching is me in some way and I never seem to make it onto the beach, perched behind the break, resisting with all my might, putting off the inevitable plunge into what lies beyond these chains that hold me back. What is inside of me wanting to get out? What is lurking in the shadows, behind the stage curtains, out of the beams of light that flood the stage in front of me? Where is my mask to hide my nakedness in it all?

Because this is the most vulnerable I have ever felt. I am the shivering that makes the goose bumps on my skin. I am the wind making my teeth chatter. I am also the throbbing warmth coursing through my veins, and it is something soft to land on. Like the comfortable idea that makes it feel OK to look in the mirror and watch time strip you slowly of your youthful skin, watch the sparkle in your eyes die like a flickering candle in the breeze, watch the life disappear like waving goodbye to an old friend that you really didn't get to know.

Maybe I had it right way around after all... this circus we call 'reality' was actually the show, and I was just a tech helping to make it happen from the safety of the dark spaces behind it all. And the swirling cacophony of my dreams was where reality lay, stripped to its essence and lying naked on the floor in front of me. How would I ever know the difference?

You could be there and not be there at the SAME fucking time, is this how it's meant to work? Could events just keep on resonating unabated, with no cure, no relief from the relentless dribble falling from the side of my mouth, the mountains of words spoken a mere smokescreen to the cry of my soul as it struggles to be heard? Would I see that hairy hand coming through the broken window forever? Would I hear the sledgehammer come crashing down as background music to my whole life? Would I feel the terror every time I got stressed or felt like I was under siege? Maybe that was it, I thought, *under siege.* That's how I've felt most of my life, bracing myself for the inevitability of the first blow. Trapped in some way, trapped in that moment.

An overwhelming feeling of gratitude comes over me, gratitude for it all, for everything that had happened, for everyone I was able to love, for every stinking moment that seemed a waste, for every band that strangled songs, for every half-arsed thing that had happened to me.

Then it occurs me, what I could do, how to say goodbye, how to set myself free, as the ocean wraps itself around me one more time...

Saying Goodbye
18 years ago

It is 2a.m, I am very drunk and I am sitting in an overstuffed chair in an apartment in South Yarra. Norma, Totto's mother, has gone to bed and now it is just myself, Totto and Marianno, who is here to ensure Totto doesn't do something bad to himself. They have been friends since childhood. Marianno is now a psychiatrist in Buenos Aires, a place he tells me has the highest rate of people in therapy outside of New York.

Mary's ashes are sitting in a clear, sealed plastic bag on the coffee table and I can't take my eyes off them. How can a human being be reduced to a small bag of dust? How could you fit Mary's wide smile into that small bag, let alone the rest of her being? Marianno is sitting next to me and we are watching Totto, who is sitting on the floor cross-legged in front of the coffee table, his head bowed. The only sound in the room is his primal sob, coming from a place few of us reach. Every gasp for breath he takes tears through me and the alcohol haze and I turn and look at Marianno. He too is crying and takes the hand I have held out to him.

We had been on a delirious bender for a week, stumbling from one bar to another, and somehow the massive intake of scotch had not even taken the edge off the pain, nor had it taken the frozen, dead stare off Totto's face. All it seemed to be doing was dulling the world around us, draining the colour from it, reducing our world to an opaque grey, not unlike Melbourne's famous winter drizzle. Not even the rain could commit in Melbourne... We had walked through blackened, shiny streets, through drizzly rain that insinuated itself on your face like a drunken, effeminate slap. We had walked through crowds of commuters with the life sucked out of them, down dull suburban streets with only the barking of dogs to punctuate our nocturnal wanderings. With the drinking came a belligerent incomprehension at nearly everything we came across. Respite came in the form of record stores, bookshops and bars. Marianno, in a gesture of friendship, bought me a Miles Davis CD called 'On the Corner' in one shop, which would later become a source of inspiration as I sat down of a night-time and made a scale model of the house I was going to build. Totto had found a rare collection of Kerouac's live performances, reading his machine gun prose to musical accompaniment. He gave it to me, saying, 'You are meant to have this,' and I grasped that box set like one of my children as we crossed a busy road. Nothing could have separated me from it. In my hands was the friendship that leapt out of the fires of grief and I was never, ever going to let it go.

I pulled one great Australian CD after another out of the stacks, exclaiming wildly each time,

"Oh, you've GOTTA to have this one too!"

From the Saints via Paul Kelly to Nick Cave via the Birthday Party, to Hunters and Collectors into Midnight Oil, Yothu Yindi, Warumpi Band, Coloured Stone via the Divinyls, into Weddings, Parties, Anything, Hoodoo Gurus, Triffids, The Reels, Mental as Anything, the Cruel Sea and finally to the Dirty Three.

There was clarity about things, about everything, and yet I could barely walk straight. This grief seemed to peel the lid off it all. I could see people's spirits underneath their charcoal grey suits. I could sense the madness just below the surface, beneath the robotic, blank faces that surrounded us. I would watch the tightness in Totto's shoulders as he walked ahead of us, somehow the crowd made a space for him every time so he didn't even need to break his drunken slur of a walk. Maybe they sensed the dark place he was in, or maybe, for an instant they saw the dead stare of someone with nothing left to lose, nothing left to live for. Someone who knew what living really meant and who had lost it all.

Now he sits on the floor in the howling early morning moment, his wife's ashes on the table next to him, the heavy marble casket he has brought with him from Argentina on the floor in front of him. He is cleaning the casket with a soft cloth and I watch the gentleness in his movement, the circular sweeps he is making that just touch the surface, the head that sinks lower with each swipe. He pulls a small jewellery box from his pocket and places it on the table next to Mary's ashes. He puts down the cloth and, with one hand holding it, opens the box with the other, revealing the gold plaque we had had made somewhere over the last two or four drunken days and nights. Out of the other pocket he takes out a tube of supa-glue and places that on the table next to the plaque, the plaque bearing his wife's name, date of birth and date of death.

I am still holding Marianno's hand and he gives it a squeeze and we both stifle our feelings and distil them into the firm, almost desperate handhold. And we remain silent. I think about the guttural screams that have been coming from Totto's room of a night time, I think of the loud, low thud as he puts his drunken fist through another wall, cracking bones he wouldn't even register had broken for weeks.

He reaches for the plaque, knocking the glue over on the way. He holds it between two fingers, turning it around and around, like someone who is seeing gold dance in the light for the first time. He places the plaque very gently onto the lid of the casket, then picks up the glue and removes the cap. He picks up the plaque again and this time his hand is trembling as he turns it over and squeezes some glue onto it, turns it back over again and holds it dead centre in front of the casket about two inches below the top. His shaking hand finally musters enough resolve to push the plaque into contact with the marble and manages to put it on straight despite the shaking hands and quivering lips. He picks up the cloth and wipes the gold plaque like he is wiping tears from the eyes of a child.

Mary's remains sit on the coffee table, a grey lump wrapped in plastic and I think of her last gasp before the car they were in smashed into the back of a tractor in the cold dark night of her last moment. I see her knowing smile, I see the benign acceptance, I see her mischievous grin, I hear the well chosen words leaving her mouth to form another great insight, I see her hand holding my daughter's as they walk to the park together, Cass's thin, wispy blond hair hanging around her like a halo. I see her terrified and bewildered expression as she hugs her frail, sick little sister – my wife – and tries not to knock the colostomy bag around her waist. I see those blue eyes so full of wisdom and life fill with awe as she plays with my daughter and listens to her wildly imaginative stories, nodding and exclaiming 'really?' whilst sneaking a smirk at Em as she lies on the couch bracing her emaciated self against the wall of pain that surrounded her.

I see her with her friend Cheryl as they discuss sexual politics and the union movement, existentialism, Marxism, whilst smoking big joints and downing cold beers on hot summer nights, nodding through the haze of smoke. I see the quirky style she had, the way she could throw together an outfit from second hand clothes, piling layer upon layer until she was a fluid representation of all that had been. I see her life lived, her spirit stretched thin across all those she loved, like a warm coat you pull tight around you as the cold wind blows through the city streets; gusts of the cold heart of humanity that threaten to dull you into a mindless stupor that only death can alleviate.

I see her riding pillion with Totto, wrapped around him, her head resting on his back in slumber as he leans his Ducati into another corner, nostrils flaring as he twists open the throttle. I see the thirst for life, and she had only taken the smallest sip. I see her waiting for the kettle to boil as the cruel dawn light pierced through the kitchen window and Totto typed madly away in the next room, page after page of poetry dripping with the juices of passion, the edges singed and blackened by the flames of the truly mad. They, too, had had a layer of shit removed early in life, revealing the chains that imprison us all. And she saw the chains, that's for sure.

I see the cigarette smoke exhaled from her lungs to make room for more words to be formed as we debated the art of telling stories with film. Was there anything left to say? we would ask ourselves as joints were passed between us and ash was spilled to the floor to join all the ideas we had given life to, another layer to be ground into the carpet.

I see the children she never had, the veranda with the armchair she never sat in to watch them play, the films she never made, the words that never got written. And I see the paralysis that has seized Totto's heart, maybe forever.

Some kind of numbness overtakes me as I watch Totto slide the lid off the casket, the heavy marble making an ominous scraping sound. I hear the thud as he slides it to the ground and the clunk as he rests it on an angle up against the side of the casket.

Totto reaches over and picks up his wife's ashes with both hands and pulls them to his chest and I hear his tears landing on the plastic. He is not making a sound but his body is trembling as he places her gently down inside the casket. It seems like a year has passed before his two hands come back out and the left hand seeks out the lid. I look at Marianno, his eyes bloodshot and swollen behind his thick glasses. He squeezes my hand and the numbness dissipates almost instantly and a flood of emotion rises up inside me as Totto's trembling body unleashes an almighty howl of pain, the intensity of which makes the childbirth howls of my wife, and my desperate screams in the hospital, seem like whimpers of discomfort.

I release my sweaty hand from Marianno's grip and lean forward in my chair. I hold my head in my hands and I stare at my friend saying goodbye to his love, I watch him wipe the casket one more time with that soft cloth before it falls from his hands towards the floor in slow-mo, like the cricket balls of my youth. Time seems to be lurching along reluctantly, from second to second, as I see his hand in mid air, the cloth seemingly frozen between him and the floor, as we all were, in the insanity brought on by grief, in the slurry pre-dawn moment, in this room bereft of dreams, in this city with its cold, dull heart.

And from where I sat I could hear the faint rumblings of a heart beat...

The Release
6 months ago

The gurgling of the espresso machine snaps me out of my dreamy state and I walk over towards the kitchen to shut it off. I realise I am naked when I get to the stove. I notice I have two cups laid out and a surge of fear hits me. I turn around and look through the dining room to the lounge, where to my surprise there is a woman with light brown hair passed out on her stomach on the mattress that is my bed, her naked body splayed out like she might have passed out immediately after sex and maintained the last position. I struggled to remember her name, I struggled to remember last night, I struggled to remember waking up. I struggled.

My head is pounding and my mind does its level best to race through the myriad possibilities of how she got here, how we got here, to me making coffee whilst the morning sun poured menacingly through the windows and splashed itself all over the floor.

Fuck, what day is it? I lurch over to the fridge to get some milk when I see the empty tequila bottle on the bench and some sort of platter of food that didn't get eaten. In my daze I pause to watch the thousands of ants that covered the platter and am sort of pleased that at least it was getting eaten. The semi-sundried tomatoes have been pretty much demolished already and they had moved on to the camembert cheese that was now a crusty liquid lump in the middle of the platter, surrounded by soggy biscuits, surrounded by an outer ring of limp baby spinach leaves. *Did I make that?*

I open the fridge door and receive the first head rush for my trouble. Luckily I am holding onto the door or else I would've been face down on the floor. And it was a slate floor, not a very forgiving surface. I wait for the blackness to fade out like the end of an old silent movie and when it did I am relieved to discover myself reaching for the carton of milk. I eye off the jug of water next to it and pull them both out.

Sometime later I find myself snapping out of another dream state to the sound of a Berocca dissolving in a glass of water. I feel my body. My hips and butt cheeks are stiff and feel kind of bruised on the inside and my legs struggle to keep me upright. My arms feel like I have shovelled concrete all day.

Snatches of images are flying through my head as if propelled by the seemingly endless throb that pervades it. I remember watching a woman taking off her retro fake fur coat and walking towards me in a silver evening gown, a mischievous, sexy grin on her face. I saw an ashtray overflowing and pieces of spent lemon spread across the coffee table. I heard acid jazz coming out of the speakers. I heard laughing, I saw a head being thrown backwards in mirth and various other theatrical gestures. *Did I work last night?* I look over my shoulder at the sleeping woman, dredging my memory for a name, a context, to no avail.

The Berocca has stopped fizzing and I gulp it down like my life depends on it, scooping the undissolved remnants up with my finger and sucking them off and then I am staring at my finger. I see her licking the same finger and then sucking it into her mouth suggestively. I see her dark brown eyes looking at me deliriously.

I pour the coffee into the cups and splash milk in their general direction, pile sugar into mine and ready myself for the long journey to the lounge room by taking a deep breath. I manage to make it without falling and plop the cups down roughly on the table of debris, which makes the woman stir slightly. She moans sleepily and changes position, bending her right leg up so it is level with her hips. I take a sip of coffee and take her in like it was the first time. I see her tight perfectly shaped arse raised slightly in the air, creating a lovely curve in her lower back where a tattoo lays accentuated by her posture. Her legs are long and finish in the smallest, most delicate feet I have ever seen. Maybe she's a dancer? I study the feet closely and realise a dancer's foot is rarely beautiful, let alone delicate. They're usually deformed and covered in corns, each joint a caricature of itself. Nope, she wasn't a dancer. I run my gaze up her slender back, a back that looks well toned, a yoga kind of toned. I reach her hair, a luscious bob of light brown waves that sit poised on her shoulder blades, as if waiting for the starter gun to commence bouncing in a ridiculously perfect way. *Who was this woman? And how did she end up here?*

I wish it was just binge drinking that was causing the blackouts, but it isn't. I know it isn't. I had been getting them at work doing shows, I had been getting them whilst paving, painting, splitting wood, in the shower. Luckily I hadn't had one whilst driving the long drive home every night... yet. But the binges, which seem pretty regular now, aren't helping that's for sure.

The sleepy, naked woman stirs again, then lets out a long slow... 'MMmmmmmmmmm...' whilst rolling over onto her side. As I take another sip of coffee, she opens her eyes and immediately shuts them again, groaning as the blinding, almost white, light hits her. I walk slowly over to the window, wondering why I didn't close the blinds last night. I undo the string and let the blind fall down and come to a stop just below the sill. I walk across to the other three windows and do the same.

"OK, it's safe to open your eyes now." I am standing on the fireplace hearth when she has another go, and this time, after much squinting and blinking, she makes it. She rolls onto her back and looks up at me. I sip my coffee and smile as I take her nakedness in, see her tiny breasts, not much more than a swollen nipple, staring back at me.

"Is that coffee I can smell?" looking me up and down appreciatively.

"Uh huh. On the table, just there," pointing with my eyes to the mess that lay there.

Her voice is husky and low, maybe from the chain smoking that we obviously undertook and the rawness brought on by tequila and lots of talking over loud music. It was coming back to me in little 5-second grabs. I see us dancing around each other with words for at least half the night, I see her sliding her dress strap off her shoulder, then pulling it down to reveal her rock hard nipples which she pinches and twists whilst licking her lips and looking at me. I see me grabbing her hair and pulling her head back, exposing her neck, which I am biting and sucking hard, the harder I do it, the deeper her nails dig into my back, the louder and more guttural her moans.

She sits up and I can see a wave of nausea hit her. She rubs her eyes.

"OH Fuck, that hurt! Why you wearin' sunnies? And can I have some too?"

She winks at me and a tiny smile fights through the hangover to reach her face as she picks up her coffee and takes a cautious sip, pausing with her full lips at the edge of the cup, testing the heat. I watch a little bit of colour return to her face.

"Didn't even realise I had 'em on!" taking them off and smiling down at her.

"And do you always wake your women up with coffee and a screaming, naked hard-on in their faces?"

Another thing I was unaware of.

"It's OK, hun, leave 'em on, it's kinda kinky. Anonymous, naked guy wearing sunnies and standing over my bed with a big hard-on... mmmm, yep, that'll do... Oh fuck, my head hurts, what did we do last night? And while I'm at it, who are you?"

"I was about to ask you the same question!"

We both laugh. I put the sunnies back on and give her a big, crazy grin, and coupled with the grey hair sticking out at all angles and the silver three day growth I must've looked pretty wild and possibly a touch crazy. *Fuck it,* I thought, *just go with it, what have you got to lose?*

"And why are my hips and pussy so sore, mister?"

I attempt to walk around her like a prowling cat but it comes off more like a lecherous stagger.

"Don't know, anonymous lady, but my body feels like it has done four marathons back to back. I think I pulled a thrust muscle at some point last night, it hurts to flex my butt cheeks!"

"Doesn't seem to have affected your cock much, he seems like he is ready for more..."

She sips her coffee and pulls a cigarette out of a discarded packet on the floor near the bed, lights it, squints to avoid the smoke getting in her eyes, looks at me, then blows the smoke out in one, long stream towards the ground, coughs loudly, then spits into a nearby ashtray.

I am still prowling around her and sipping my coffee, the thought of a cigarette enough to make my head start pounding again and turn the prowl to a theatrical stagger. I can see the coffee table and I focus my dim-witted brain on it. I make it there and attempt to sit my naked butt down on the edge. I miss and hit the floor, she is laughing before I even hit. I lean my elbow on the table to break my fall and up-end it on me, the ashtray and spent lemons sliding off and landing on my chest and stomach.

"Now, that was hilarious! Do it again, do it again!" she shrieks, and then she is holding her head in her hands and moaning.

"Oh fuck, that hurt, " she groans. She reaches into her bag and pulls out her sunnies and puts them on.

"Aah, that's better." She looks over at me lying on my back covered in cigarette ash and lemon peel.

"That did the trick, hey? Your little brother has gone back to sleep," pointing to my cock, "and I am not surprised either, given the work out he had last night!"

She runs a hand down her leg absentmindedly whilst sucking more smoke down into her lungs.

I stare up at the ceiling and hope that all the knots in the wood stop looking like demented rabbits soon. I clear my throat of a layer of phlegm.

"Well, here we are then."

"Yes, two anonymous people wearing sunglasses inside, naked, hungover or maybe still drunk, cause I don't recall sleeping much at all since we fucked for hours and hours, you're lying in last night's rubbish and keep blacking out and I'm not even sure what MY name is!"

"I'm pleased not to have met you," my voice like hot tar stuck to your shoe.

She smiles at me,

"Whoever you are, I like you and I think you should brush that shit off you and roll on over here... I think I wanna make you my bitch!"

She stubs out her cigarette, blows the remaining smoke out loudly and lays herself down on the bed again, slowly opening her legs and sliding her left hand up and down the entrance to her pussy.

Each roll I make is like a rollercoaster and after the third roll I leave my body and float above us. I watch my hammered body make the final roll onto the mattress where this crazy lady with no name, that I had no memory of seeing before, was lying, playing with herself. If her lips weren't a cracked, dry shadow of their former selves she probably would've been whistling.

A large chunk of time goes missing and I wake to find myself curled up in a ball in the middle of the room. Still naked, still wearing sunnies. I can see her asleep on the bed in the same position I first saw, on her stomach with one leg bent in half and pulled up to her hips. Shit, did any of that just happen? My head is pounding again, my eyes blurry. I sit up and search for my phone, miraculously it is within reach, upside down on the floor near the sound system. I grab it and struggle to get it working, then realise I have it the wrong way around, correct it and the screen lights up. The screen tells me it is Saturday the 10th August and the time is 10.30 a.m. I let this information seep into my brain, into the sludge of dead brain cells. Then I remember.

"OH FUCK!" Suddenly wide awake, I look around me. Fuck, the prospective buyers of the house are coming here today at 11 for a second look. FUUUCK, the room looks like a hedonistic bomb has hit it, how the hell did this happen? I spring up and start frantically clearing the shit off the table, open the fire place door and start throwing stuff in. Anything. Everything. I pick up half a dozen empty glasses and rush over to the kitchen, dropping one of them on the way, it smashing into a hundred pieces and spreading itself on the floor in front of me. I wince when I feel the first shard tear through the skin on my heel but continue on regardless.

"FUCK!" I scream, as I limp over to the sink and put the remaining glasses there. I hear the nameless woman stirring and saying,

"What the fuck's going on?"

"People comin' soon to check out the house again... in half an hour!"

I limp across to the door and open it, followed by every other door and window, keen to blow the stale smell of sex and last night's party out, out into the crisp morning.

"I guess me lying here naked isn't a great vibe then?"

"Nah, probably not," my voice pregnant with understatement.

I spit through pain as I pull the shard of glass out of my heel and look at the trail of crimson red blood that I have spread across the floor.

She gets up off the mattress and stretches, locking her hands above her head and arching her back like a cat.

"How long we got?"

"20 minutes."

"Shit, we better move fast then!"

***

Half an hour later we are sitting at the kitchen table waiting for the coffee to be ready, and have even managed to put clothes on. I can hear the familiar sound of car tyres on the gravel driveway so I look at her and say,

"OK, we're on!"

She brushes her wild wavy hair off her face and says,

"Still wanna make you my bitch," and winks at me as we hear the knock on the door.

Anonymous girl gets up as I go to the door and exclaims,

"I really like this place, it's so open and the view is spectacular!" in her best South Yarra accent. I open the door and greet the couple standing there. She is still going on about the house, gesticulating a lot and talking about the changes she would make if she decides to buy it. I am sort of enjoying her performance but also freaked out she will go too far and blow the sale. I look sheepishly at the couple who have just driven up from Melbourne with a cheque book in their hands.

"Um, sorry about this, she rang an hour ago and said she simply had to see the house now," I say apologetically.

"It's OK," she chimes in, "I'm done. This place is fabulous. I will be in contact soon," walking towards me with her hand out to shake mine, "Mr...?"

There is an awkward silence as I struggle to remember my name. She winks at me and smiles cheekily, and I can't help but smile back.

"You can call me Tony," I say, remembering at last.

She takes my hand as I say,

"And it was nice to meet you… aah… Ms...?"

"And you can call me Stella," she retorts playfully.

I watch her walk off toward her car, attempting to fling the fake fur over her shoulders, and failing, swinging that ass and knowing I am looking. I smile to myself.

It is going to be a good day.

A Desert and a Slide Guitar
4 years ago

Bazza does a few slow circuits of the feral cat tree and every now and then he taps one of the 'dead' cats, making it swing gloomily in front of him. Each time he does it his face lights up even more and from where I stand the childlike wonder on his face is an eerie counterpoint to the death mask make-up he has applied. It's a pity the audience can't get this close to the action, trapped in their plush seats in the auditorium, in their state of distant reverence. If they could, they would see the texture on Bazza's face lit beautifully by two amber lights 6 metres above his head and another 4 in the auditorium ceiling cavity. They would see the beads of desperation running down over his chin and dripping onto the floor in front of him. They would see the actor appearing through the cracks in the make-up, they would see a man struggling to choose which 'reality' suits him best. Or perhaps he will float precariously between the two, Harry and Bazza, destined to drift forever between the winds, neither here nor there, real or a figment of someone else's imagination.

There is the sound of a slide guitar coming gently over the speakers, playful runs of notes ending in long, drawn out resonating chords that send a chill through me. The reverb is dripping off the sound, giving the scene an aural eeriness that no amount of lighting and acting can express and soon I am floating on the notes, drifting across the chords like they were a velvet walkway to nirvana. The music swells and fills the room, the reverb pulled right back, leaving the sound naked and raw. You can hear the attack of each note like a cold knife into tight flesh, and each chord physically cuts through Bazza, weakening his resolve and dropping him to his knees. He clasps his hands together and puts them on his chest, like he is praying, except his hands have formed fists and I can see the whites of his knuckles as he squeezes them hard together. His voice comes out croaky, unsure, bewildered, vulnerable.

"Haven't ever prayed before big fella, so go easy on me, OK?

The guitar fades into the distance, a delicate fade that seems to deliver Bazza's words into the room.

"Fact is, up 'til now I couldn't have given a fuck whether you exist or not... never found you at the bottom of a bottle or two, never found you anywhere, not even after my footy team won the grand final so I figured, 'fuck you mate', and blundered through 45 years of my life without even being aware I was alive... and now... now I'm here in the desert kneeling under a tree full of dead cats hanging upside down in this dusty moonlight and to be honest mate, I'm scared... can I call you 'mate'? Or does a self-flagellating priest appear before me and turn his steel encrusted whip on me whilst secretly getting off on it, hey? Sorry mate, but your self-appointed representatives are a pretty fucked up lot. It looks like suppressing emotions doesn't work out too well, hey mate? All those kiddy-fiddlers that lived under your roof for so long, hiding the awful truth of their hypocrisy, your hypocrisy. Is that what you call 'free will' is it? The free will to fuck as many people up as possible in the name of God, yeah you, you miserable piece of shit!"

Bazza pauses mid barrage to blow his nose football style, holding one nostril and firing a wet web of snot all over the base of the tree. The lights capture the fine spray coming off it as it flies into the air and then wafts slowly down to the stage floor. He wipes the rest on his sleeve.

"And now I am waking up mate, and where the fuck are you now? Someplace I s'pose, fucking nowhere to be seen, that's where…"

The dead cat lanterns start to glow softly, a deep, dim amber, not enough to throw light on Bazza's face but just enough to be noticeable. The overhead lights dim down really slowly and are replaced with a very low, deep blue light and when that is done the 100 dead cat lanterns come into their own with an accompanying swell of a deep low chord from the slide guitar, which goes up in pitch as the lights fade up, illuminating the serene bewilderment building on Bazza's face. I can hear the audience gasp in awe at the scene before them, a man on his knees in front of one of the most beautiful and gothic sets I have ever seen, lit so effectively that the set seems to be lifted off the stage and into another realm, floating eerily over the heads of the open-mouthed audience.

"Where are you now, asshole?" Bazza screams to the tree, his head falling down into his lap and when it lands he lets out a tear soaked wail of pain. The guitar bounces off his wail and launches into a poetic and raw solo that almost takes my legs out from under me, taking me to a place no words can go. If the human spirit had a sound, then this would be it. A slide guitar in the desert, a tired old soul on his knees with nowhere left to go.

It is absolutely silent in the theatre except for the sniffing and coughing of Bazza, the sound echoing into this old building and settle with all the other emotions that the creaky old girl was carrying.

"Where... are... you... now?" Bazza groans whilst coughing deeply, a wracking cough that sound like his insides are coming out.

"Where is anyone?" he croaks.

I am metres from Bazza and the tree as he slumps down even more, crawls over to the thick trunk and drags himself into a sitting position, up against it. Now he is facing the audience and he is staring up into the tree, glowing dead cats hanging by their tails all around him, his face sliced up by the cats' shadows. A thin band of light cuts across him diagonally from above, tears across his face and down his shoulder and onto the floor in line with where I am standing.

"Wow, this is the most beautiful tree I have ever seen. And look at the stars! Fuck, how could there be so many, how come I've never really noticed them before. In all my 65 years, where was I looking instead?"

He looks from side to side, then turns so he is looking at the audience.

"Aah there you are, love! But how did you find me all the way out here?"

Muriel's voice comes over the P.A.

"Baz, most people can smell you a mile away and I, well, I always know where you are!"

The audience laughs, feeling the tension ease.

"Y'know Muriel, I'm glad you came. Not a bad spot, hey?"

"Yeah, bewdiful Baz. What ya doin' all the way out here in the desert you old crazy bastard? Didn't even tell me you were going!"

"There's a lot of things I didn't tell you, love. After so many years of talking without words I had forgotten how to use them. There's so much I didn't say, didn't realise I even felt. And now I feel wide-awake for the first time in my life. Muriel, listen! ... I love you, I have always loved you, I love the verbal banter, I love sitting on the porch with you, sinkin' beers. I loved the calm, easy understanding and I took it all for granted to the point where you were so much a part of me you weren't even there. I want to say I'm sorry Muriel, you are the love of my life, and I didn't even know it..."

"Oh you fuckin' romantic fool, I love you too Baz, with all my heart. And I always will, not matter what sort of shit comes out of your mouth!"

"I think I'm dying Muriel."

"See, there you go again!"

A howl of laughter from the crowd.

The sound of Muriel's voice fades. Bazza looks back up at the tree and closes his eyes. He is gasping for breath now, I can hear the raspy, tortured attempts, but the death rattle has a hold on him now.

The sound of a busy pub fades up over the P.A., Bazza's local, and you can hear the chings and rings of the poker machines, a race-caller is yelling excitedly, '...and coming into the straight it's Sugar Daddy a head in front of Freudian Slip, followed by Buckley's Hope and bursting out of the pack it's Valiant Charger...' over the top of men muttering and the clink of the beer tap springing back to home position.

Bazza's eyes open slowly as he says,

"Go, Valiant Charger!"

He raises a fist feebly into the air, then drops it to his side, stares up at the tree one last time.

"Fuckin' beautiful tree, this one..."

The pub sounds fade and the slide guitar returns. I watch as the cat lanterns fade down over a minute, the slide guitar a sparse thing with as much silence as music. Bazza's eyes close, he is smiling, his legs splayed out and forming a 'V' as the stage goes to black, the slide guitar surging quickly, a flurry of high order harmonics, then subsiding as the house curtains close and the audience erupt into wild applause. Some are whistling their appreciation. I watch Harry stand up almost like he is stepping out of Bazza's dead skin and into his own again. He looks back fondly at the place where Bazza had been sitting, then turns quickly holding out his hands as the other actors join him on stage for the bows. They are all smiling, feeling the buzz of electricity they had created, that we all had a part in. The curtain opens and they are flooded with adulation and they all look at the audience for a moment and the first group bow begins. I peer through a crack in the curtains and see that the audience are on their feet and the applause fills the room, building to a frenzy when Harry makes his bow. He walks forward and bows to the audience as Harry the medieval jester and does a little skip on the way back. The curtain closes again and as I bag up the curtains legs in preparation for the bump out, I watch as the actors go in for a group hug in the darkness, in the shadow of a hundred dead cats hanging from a tree...

The Raffle
20 years ago

I am slumped in a chair in the plastics ward watching a lady mopping the floor. The squeak of her shoes and the swish swish of the wet mop on the tiled floor has me in a mesmerised state. I have been listening to my recordings, my stir-crazy hospital ramblings, and wondering how close a man can get to madness before it's too late to get back, back to the general state of hysteria that masquerades as reality. I stop the tape and pull a fresh one out of my gown pocket, insert it into the player and hit 'record' and soon I am listening in great detail to this anonymous lady, with her percussive movements, and the distant sounds of a busy hospital ward. Through the headphones there seems to be so much more detail, more texture to the sounds than my naked ear can discern. It's like the sensitivity has been taken up to full, and I like it this way.

I look at my arm all bandaged up and notice the infection that won't seem to go away soaking through the bandages. I attempt to make a fist with my right hand and all I can muster is a few millimetres of movement back and forth. I cannot feel my lower arm and hand at all and the doctors won't give me a guarantee that it will get any better, indicating I am damn lucky to have an arm at all. From where I sit I can see all the way to the end of the corridor at both ends. I can see the distorted, surreal

Christmas tree laden with the refuse of our hospital experiences and I can see the double doors at the other end as they swing open and a cluster of doctors in white coats stride through. The rounds have begun. I sit up slowly as they walk past and nod slightly to them as the young interns struggle to keep pace with the older, balder, greyer one at the head of the pack, his stride a confident one, a cluster of files in one hand, gesticulating with the other. They turn right into a room with 6 beds in it holding patients with various parts of their bodies missing or heavily bandaged. I struggle to rise up out of my slumped posture, eventually I manage it and head off to my bed like a good boy so I can wait for the gods of this place to bless me with their presence. I leave the recorder going and listen as the mopping fades and is replaced by my shuffling steps.

When I enter the room Pete sits up in bed exclaiming,

"Tone, where ya been, mate, hardly seen you lately?"

I take one headphone out of my ear.

"Huh? Aah, you know, checking the place out, watching it all happen. How ya doin' anyway?"

"Fucked if I know, they've got me on morph now so everything's just a big dream…"

"Yeah, you seem to be sleeping a lot."

"Well, what else can I do mate?" He holds his fingerless hands up to me.

"Can't even read a fuckin' book and these movies you gave me are worse than death! What's with this shit?"

I laugh and hit 'stop' on the recorder, pull the other earphone out.

"Well, what would you rather see?"

"I dunno, somethin' that doesn't put me to sleep like your shit does," pointing to the stack of videos Totto had brought in for me.

They were all classics. Blonde Venus, Rear Window, Johnny Guitar, La Dolce Vita, Blood Simple, all great movies but not Pete's cup of tea it seemed.

"You know, like, you got any porn?"

I smile at him and say,

"I'll see what I can do," and just as I turn around the doctor gods are entering the room and looking at my empty bed. The older one looks a little confused.

"Whoops," I say to Pete and give him a wink and walk on over to my bed, excusing myself as I make my way through the wall of white coats, hamming it up with John Cleese style over the top grating politeness. I make it to the bed and as I lie down I say,

"Hang on a sec!" and proceed to pull at my hair to make it stand up, slacken my jaw so I looked drugged and put the earphones back in, press 'record' and say,

"OK, I'm 'right now... proceed!"

The greying doctor clears his throat and stifles a smirk, the only one to see my antics, the rest of them feverishly writing notes in their little pads. When he clears his throat they all look up, scan my body until they see the 'injury' and focus their gaze on that.

"This patient has a..."

"Um, excuse me," I interrupt, "This patient has a name, it's Tony, what's yours?" I inquire, smiling, hearing my voice in the headphones, nice and clear.

A little shocked, he replies with,

"Um, it's Dr Patten."

Looking at his name badge,

"Can I call you John? I mean, you've had your hands inside my arm, I figure we could skip the polite shit now."

A touch exasperated now, he replies,

"OK, OK, yes, yes!"

I look around at the interns and one or two of them are sneaking little grins and looking furtively around the bed I am lying in.

"OK, great, glad we got that sorted," I say, "now, what's on your mind John?"

He goes into his spiel, about 30 seconds of medical phrases I had become familiar with and I notice his tone changes, it almost has a conspiratorial whisper about it. He then clears his throat.

"Aah Mr... aah, Tony?"

"Yep, right here John."

"I have conferred with the nurses and I can't see why we can't send you home. How would you like to spend Christmas with your family and loved ones? We can't tell you how much use of your arm you will regain. In a lot of ways, it's up to you now. Christmas Eve tomorrow, let's see if we can't clean that infection up and send you home with a strong course of antibiotics. How does that sound?"

I didn't expect this and it has floored me, my smart-alec layer dripping off me and replaced with tears as I think of my girls opening their presents, still in their pyjamas, sleepy looks of surprise on their faces. I don't answer him. I just look at him, grinning like an idiot.

"OK, well, all the best then, Tony, and let's hope we never see you up here again," and then he is walking over to Pete's bed, the interns following like frightened sheep.

A tear hits my recorder as I sniff back the phlegm that has filled my nose. I press the 'stop' button and stare past the doctors and Pete, through the window and out onto the street. I see myself getting into the passenger seat of our car, my wife helping me whilst our daughters sit happily in their car seats in the back, kicking their legs. I see us going over Gap Hill and me looking in the side mirror to watch the city disappear in an instant. Then I see us driving down the driveway to our amazing house in the bush, and it is then that I see my Ducati parked under the veranda.

I get up out of bed, rustle through the drawers until I find some coins and a minute or so later I am standing next to the Christmas tree, the public phone handset to my ear, listening to Totto's phone ringing. Eventually he picks it up and groggily answers.

"Totto, it's Tony, sorry to wake you up but I need your help. I need a couple of porn movies for tonight. Don't ask why, OK? And the big one. Could you go and get my bike off my fucking veranda, just take it to your place or something. I don't wanna see it mate, it'll break me up to see what I may never be able to ride again. Can you do that for me?"

"Yeah, sure, are they letting you out? When?"

"Tomorrow night, Christmas eve."

"Awesome, consider it done, I'll see ya later. Ciao!"

I hang up and stare at the surreal Christmas tree for a while. Then I smile to myself and head back to the room just as the doctors are leaving a fairly stunned looking Pete. I walk up to him.

"What's up?"

He looks up at me.

"Can't believe it. After all this time here, now they reckon I'm fit enough to have my hip replaced.

252

Scheduled the op for the day after Boxing Day...
fuckin' hell, Tone, looks like I'm getting out soon too!"
   "Well, we should definitely celebrate!"

***

   Later that night I quietly wheel Pete and the
TV trolley out onto the balcony. Pete has put the word
out, and those that are able to, follow us out. Fred the
throat cancer victim has a bottle of scotch, which he
produces from under his gown. We all rip into it,
someone passes a joint around and soon enough we
are all laughing at one of Fred's jokes,
   "What's the difference between a blonde and
a bowling ball? You can only get three fingers in a
bowling ball!"
   He holds the gaping hole in his throat, his
voice comes out like a Dalek from Dr Who, except
when he laughs it all goes bad for him and his face
turns blue as he struggles to breathe.
   The first porn movie is up and running and
after a few minutes of some chick trying to suck a
massive cock and failing I get bored and stare out at
the shimmering lights of suburbia. There is a gentle
hum coming from the few cars that are scattered
along Royal Parade and an empty tram rattles its way
towards the big roundabout. *The strike must be over*, I
think, I *wonder who won?* but I already know the
answer as I reflect on the muted power of the unions
in the face of an overblown and all powerful
government that signed a contract with a French
ticketing machine company that in turn is keeping the
politicians in lobsters and champagne. So much for a
socialist government. So much for the now
unemployed trammies.

The chick is now attempting to straddle the monster cock and the boys all seem pretty happy about it, egging her on like they are watching a horse race. The bottle is almost empty as I see Pete take a good, long pull on it and laugh as it slips out of his tenuous grasp. He shrieks as the chick finally succeeds and is riding the monster cock like she is one of the jockeys. I sit down next to Pete and look at the dulled wonder in his eyes, his toothless grin the perfect counterpart to his scraggily beard.

He leans towards me, puts one of his stump hands on my shoulder and says,

"Good idea Tone. One last bender, why not? You're a good bloke Tone, and I wanna tell you something..."

He takes another pull on the bottle, then coughs and splutters for a while. He wipes his mouth with the back of his stump and and says,

"I'm not gonna make it Tone. They know it and I know it. I just wanted to tell you that meeting you made my year, mate. Fuck it, it made my decade, and I just wanna tell you, don't ever give up on yourself like I have. You've got a family that loves you, more than I've ever had. Don't throw it away Tone. Your arm is just God's way of waking you up. Don't fall asleep again, for my sake. I want you to live the life, the best life you can... use what's happened to you to make you strong. Turn it around. Do it for me, OK mate?"

"Aah, you fuckin' drunk! What a load of bullshit!" I say with mock bravado. But deep down I am moved beyond words. Just then the door to the ward opens and two of the guys are dragging the Christmas tree out towards us, tripping drunkenly over themselves as they do, breaking into bursts of laughter each time one of them stumbles and falls, bringing the sad tree down on themselves. Finally they get it together and stand this strange symbol up on its prosthetic legs, smoothing the branches down as if trying to repair the damage they had caused. Behind them lies a trail of broken branches and our twisted ornaments. One of them yells,

"Bit of shoosh please!"

Everyone falls silent, leaving only the sound of the moaning chick and the hum of the traffic.

"We would like to announce the winner of the raffle. You all know and love him even though he's a gnarly old drunk. Pete, as winner of this raffle you are required to adorn yourself with your prizes, so if you'd like to come forward the ceremony can begin!"

He sways as he is talking and has picked up the large Christmas hamper, which he throws over the edge of the balcony and a few seconds later we hear it crash and disintegrate. Somebody has turned up the sound from the video and some really cheesy disco music is mixed with the moaning of the chick and the grunting of the man with the massive cock as Pete wheels himself over to the tree, his drunken grin stretched wide across his face as the man tapes the first prosthetic leg onto Pete's shoulder whilst the other guy puts the prosthetic arm where Pete's leg should've been.

I grin, a wide full grin. It just makes sense, I think, as the sound of an ambulance siren makes its way through the night towards us...

A Desert and a Slide Guitar
4 years ago

We are lowering the dead cat tree onto the ground when Harry appears at the side of stage, an old Gladstone bag in his left hand. The flyman calls the move and those of us on the floor grab a branch or a trunk and guide it gently to the floor. The cat lanterns have already been removed and are lying in a pile just off stage. The crew starts dismantling it and I give the all-clear to the flyman to take the flyline out that was holding the tree. I then walk over to Harry with my hand outstretched. He is pushing his wild, grey hair off his face and attempting to smooth it out when he sees me coming, a grin from ear to ear on both our faces. I take his hand and give it a good, firm squeeze and say,

"Harry it's been an absolute pleasure to meet and hang out with you!"

We hold the handshake as Harry replies,

"Took the words right out of my mouth, Tone!"

"Wow, that must be a first for you?"

He laughs.

It's easy to say goodbye for us, we do it nearly every day. For him it is a new venue, a new crew every few days. For me it's a different show and different actors and crew, and after a while you see the beauty in the short connection with no expectations, except to be real, be who you are, in the moment. Harry wasn't going to say 'let's keep in touch', as he knew it doesn't work that way. The young ones did that, adding Facebook friends like a junky adding holes to his arm and sometimes it did work that way. But rarely. We'd had a good connection and now it was over. Simple. But I can't seem to let go of his hand or stop grinning at him.

"So, where next for you?" I ask.

"Some place called Horsham, Tone, no fucking idea where that is and all I can hope is that there is a decent bookshop nearby."

I picture the sleepy town of Horsham, the cold, empty streets at 8p.m., the redneck bigotry simmering just below the surface, the smell of sheep shit on the boots of the locals.

"If you've got a day off, get yourself to a place called Talbot. It's a couple of hours from Horsham and it's got the coolest bookshop outside of Melbourne. It's a little ghost town, with grand old buildings from the gold rush days and hardly any people. You'll love it!"

"Talbot. Talbot. OK, will do Tone. As long as you do something for me."

"Sure Harry."

"Get the fuck out of here, my friend, you've waited long enough now. I can see it in your eyes, can hear it in your words. Don't waste too much more time in this place playing the role of Head Tech. There's so much more out there for you..."

And with that he releases my hand, gives me a wink and walks off towards the stairwell, towards the next gig, his little brown bag, with Christ knows what inside, clasped tightly in his left hand.

***

I make it home by 1a.m. and, as usual, cannot sleep. Something about the adrenalin of the gig takes a long time to leave me and I wander aimlessly around my big, empty house for a while, remembering the last few amazing days. A few moments to hang on to, to get me through all the others. The ones that ate away at you slowly, leaving you feeling spent and used up.

Usually some late night TV did the trick, a few minutes of 'infomercials' guaranteed a deep sleep. But not tonight. I feel the urge to mark this moment somehow, but not with bourbon and a joint. I see myself turning on the outside lights and gazing out the window at the frill- necked lizard, which is lit on one side by the floodlight. A few minutes later I find myself draping fairy lights through the frill- neck and running one line down the spine of this strange sculpture I have made. Half an hour later I am running the power lead through the window and walking across to turn all the other lights off. With expectant glee I flick the switch and the lizard lights up, a dazzling contrast to the cold, dark night all around it, a shimmering array of little lights illuminating the gnarly 'mistletoe' pieces and all combining to create an eerie glow that is shrouded in a low mist. I stare in wonder at this image, I stare in wonder at my beautiful isolation, I stare in wonder at my long hibernation and realise that now, it is finally over...

Liquid Moments
1 month ago

"Dad, do you wanna keep this?" Cass asks as she holds up another vase she has found in the back of a cupboard.

I look up from what I am doing and look at the vase, realising it isn't mine, it had somehow been left by the last girlfriend. *Funny,* I thought, *she took a lot of stuff that wasn't hers to take and then leaves a vase for me. And the kind of flowers I like are already dead and don't need water or a vase, only a sharp nail driven through the stem to hold 'em on the wall...*

"Nah, Cass, it's yours if you want it, otherwise throw it in the rubbish pile."

We both look out onto the veranda where a large pile of unwanted objects lie, objects that were at some point important and have since been discarded, neglected, have gathered dust in a cupboard somewhere.

She turns it over in her hands, examining the vase, looking at the pattern, the roses inlaid in the glass, and the shape of it. From where I stand, it looks like a wine carafe. *Now, that's a useful vessel*, I think.

"Was this Lisa's, Dad?"

"Must've been."

I turn back to my piles of books and then I hear a smash outside and see Cass walking back inside with a satisfied smile on her face. I smile at her and say nothing.

I have hundreds of books laid out around me on the floor and I am slowly putting them in the strong cardboard boxes I had rescued from the recycling bin at work. Each one I pick up resonates within a time frame that seems so far away now, and as I put them away I realise I am also putting my past self away, a person I barely even recognise now. So many gems amongst them, so many words that transported me out of myself and made the human experience almost worth it. I pick up another pile and on top is a David Goodis novel called 'The Burglar'. I open it to the first page where one of the best opening lines I had ever read lay:

'Winter came in like an anarchist with a bomb.'

I remember first reading that when I was twenty and I walked around muttering '9 words!' for days. He was one of the first writers to grab me by the scruff of the neck and make me listen. There was so much shit out there, so many words flagrantly thrown at a sentence, like saturation bombing. Eventually they hope to hit the mark and if the reader was still with them they were a pulpy, mesmerised shadow of their former selves. I liked the writing that burst out of desperation, of no time left, the soul gasping for air.

There was a pile of his books amongst many others, and I silently thanked them all for what they had shown me, for what they had shown me about my young self- a man floundering and not knowing why, a numb spirit who saw no value in trying.

I had carried these books around with me for years, through various houses, and now they were being put to rest, in some ways, forever. In the early days these books were what defined me, more than

260

any of my ham-fisted actions could convey, and as I filled and then sealed each box I wondered if I would ever open their pregnant pages again.

Cass is doing the final clean up of the kitchen and I watch her silently. There is a beauty in her deft movements, the beauty of someone enjoying what they are doing and extracting a sense of satisfaction from it. And to have her here on the final day of this house is incredibly special to me. She had sat and watched me make a scale model of this house 17 years ago and I remember her and Hannah both asking those piercingly honest questions that childhood innocence manifests.

"Why are the walls not straight, Dad, and can we have a fireman's pole to slide down from our bedrooms when dinner is ready," and then, later, *"Why can't it be just a normal house, Daddy, like my friends'?"*

All I could muster as a response was stuff like, *"Daddy just isn't normal, and I'm loving every minute of it!"* which would further incite them.

And now my eldest was a young woman, paving her own way, and for her there was no sledgehammer to propel her forward, thank christ. I had made sure of that. The youngest was already off adventuring in Northern Australia, working for an Aboriginal community. She had gone as far away from the small town she grew up in as she could, and I think in some ways she had found an easy freedom in that. She was living in a third world community that no-one in Australia cared to admit to, so ingrained was our collective guilt that we like to pretend that that shit happened in Africa and Bangladesh, not in our own backyard.

Eventually we are done, the last pile of dust swept up and thrown onto the trailer with all the other rubbish, the other old lifejackets that I no longer used, now buried under plastic bags and worn out rugs and ready to go to the tip. The car has my clothes in it, and a large wooden box I had made at high school as a 14 year old – an aborted attempt at a game involving a track made of thin ply, a small ball and a piece of dowel that moved back and forth in slots in the sides and controlled the ball on the track… It kind of worked, but I got bored after the second or third game and the box, which was very strong, had served as storage for photos, mementos and an overflowing stack of journals and short stories, ever since. It had sat under a dozen beds gathering dust each time and had been pulled out occasionally to throw more onto the pile…

The 'stuff' that I possessed was now reduced to a wooden box that one person could lift. I had condensed the stuff that mattered to me, reduced it like a good soup stock, until it was the raw, exposed heart of things, a source of fuel for my fire, a place of remembering and forgetting, a place where you could watch the two dance endlessly, drunk with the pulsating rhythm of their own volition. It couldn't be any other way.

Cass is brushing herself off and walking towards me. We are outside by the cars.

"Well Dad, this is it then. Are you ready to say goodbye to her?" pointing to the house.

I take her in my arms and hug her tightly.

"Thank you, Cass, for being here for this, it means a lot to me."

"Me too Dad. Gees, I remember your little model sitting on the dining room table for, like, a year!"

I laugh and squeeze her again, then release her and hold her hands.

"We did alright, didn't we Cass?" looking out at the house, at all the years gone by in a blink of an eye.

"Yeah Dad, we did."

I watch her drive out the gate and wait for her wave and beep and I wave back. From there she can't see the tears of pure joy collecting like new friends in the corners of my eyes. I turn back to the house: the doors are locked, the paving is swept, all the random stuff gone, except the crazy sculptures. For some reason the new owners like them and had asked to keep them, even the frill necked lizard seemed poised to crouch there for a while longer. Who would've thought?

And then, I am ready, and when it comes to it, it is quite easy, much easier than I had thought it would be. I start the car, put on Dirty Three's 'Everything's Fucked' – one of my favourite tracks – put the car in gear and drive on out, up the driveway towards the gate. I take one last look through the rear-view mirror as the house slowly disappears from view. I turn left onto the dirt road that takes me to the highway. And I don't look back.

I just turn up the music and break into a huge smile.

A Beach in Thailand
Present

I know what I have to do, but how to do it? I don't even know if he is alive, let alone where he might have ended up after all these years. I wonder if he ever thinks about the night he set our world on fire, the evening of my deliverance, the end of innocence, the birth of the siege-like mentality that has occupied a place in every waking moment since... I wonder if he ever suffers regret or is his anger still burning bright? How has his life gone for him? Did he find any peace, a moment of respite from the white-hot intensity of his frustration and anger? Had he found help, or is he in denial?

The crashing waves spread themselves out on the sand and envelop me, but there is no fear left in me. I just let them hit me, and it feels great. The shore break is an explosive rumble and punctuates my thoughts, pounding them down to a fine powder and scattering them with the wind, and I struggle to retain a few grains as another flood hits me. How long have I been here? Hours? Minutes? Seconds? It doesn't matter anymore, time is of no concern to me. For the first time, it really feels like I have landed in the exquisite eternity of the now. And there is no going back. Not now. Not ever.

My mouth feels dry and sandy, my eyes sore and swollen, my ears waterlogged and raw from aural overload, my legs and arms ache from the ocean's pummelling of them. Fuck, it feels good. The beach looks like a bomb has hit it, there is shit everywhere. Next to me is a huge, twisted ball of fishing nets, larger than my log, and I wonder how I didn't end up snared on it. I sit up and look around. *Where is my log?* I scan the beach, figuring it must have finally made it, but I can't see it. I see car tyres and flip flops and plastic bags, oil drums, lumps of rope, children's broken toys, but not my log.

I look out at the ocean, just behind the break where I had last seen it rolling wilfully about. It is not there either. What has become of it? Everything else has been spat onto the beach and now the tide is going out, there is less chance I will find it with each set of angry waves. The shore break are brown balls of fury, the receding tide hollowing out the monsters before they embed themselves in the sand. They are still full of driftwood and other debris but they are getting smaller now, down to small splinters of wood you could pick up with one hand.

I stand up slowly and immediately feel dizzy so I settle for crouching on my haunches instead.

Many men I had known over the years talked about their Dad being there, but not being there. They talked about how he was busy working or out in the shed. He was absent and yet physically there. I feared for the children of Viet Nam vets, a broken wall of terror at what they had done pervading these men's lives; returning back to suburbia as ticking time bombs, exploding in the face of an entire generation, and a generation after that. Why worry about terrorism when your own government is delivering thousands of nutcases straight back into their family life like nothing had happened? How many men had become trapped in the suburban dream and were waiting to erupt out of their sheds and unleash a lifetime of confusion onto those around them? How many men were frozen and going through the motions of manhood uninitiated, without a clue in the world how to go about it? Was that what was making this world so sick and dysfunctional? Maybe in some ways I was spared a worse fate by not having the bastard there at all.

I start walking down the beach searching for my log amongst the piles of debris that had formed like plastic sand dunes all along the beach. I walk in the direction I had last seen Phee Noi and Phee Nan and I realise they were also nowhere to be seen. *Had they been here at all, or was that also a figment of my imagination? And for that matter, am I inhabiting a dream I wanted to have? For fuck's sake, why would I put myself through this, dragging myself through all these moments in my life like a kid who wanted to see the comedy movie but got the documentary instead? Why was I obsessively searching for this stupid log on this beach at 44 years of age, crying like a baby, howling and laughing like I had finally got the joke? After all these years, why would all this erupt in my face?*

For years I had glimpsed the crumbling foundation out of the corner of my eye, and when I tried to look at it straight on, it would disappear, only to reappear in the periphery of my vision, plaguing me with its presence, a presence I could only sense...

I walk past many pieces of driftwood, their bright, happy colours jumping out of the muted, faded lumps of plastic, but I am not interested now. Normally, I would pick up each piece and marvel at its wonderful transformation, from fishing boat to tortured and caressed driftwood, eaten by sea worms, barnacles and mussels attached to its surface. And I would keep just about every piece. They would often end up in a table or a sculpture I was making. But no, all I want to find is my tortured log, the only thing on this beach that makes sense to me.

I turn around and head back to where I had been immersed for so long in the log's seductive movement, hoping that being there will bring her back to me. My heart races and my chest is thumping palpably as I walk briskly along a beach that I would normally saunter along. The more I look, the less I see, until I am back to where I had been sitting, my eyes blurry from this fruitless search. And then, as my heart rate settles, I realise that to find it, I have to stop trying.

I sit down on a sandbank above where I had been grappling with my life and had not seen the signs. Or worse, sensed them but could not make them a tangible thing. Tangible like my log, like the dried tears caked on my cheeks, like the trembling that comes from somewhere so deep, it is impossible to find its source. I am out of sync, moving way faster than everything around me. Each wave that crashes thunderously onto the sand seems like a slow-mo replay. I could have run up each face and leapt off the top without getting wet. And yet my log evades me.

I look down over the beach in front of me like someone who has got to the show after it has started. Birds have started picking through the debris, gulping down plastic bottle caps, drinking straws, those small toys that come in a box of cereal, tiny flip-flops. They don't seem to realise that this isn't food. A couple of them land on the huge pile of knotted, twisted nets that I had woken up next to and have started pulling strands off and flicking them over their shoulders like they had done this a million times. They probably had. I watch them intently, these two sea gulls, their cold black eyes set against fine, white feathers, their hard beaks tearing away at the nets. They seem to be getting more frantic in their movements, maybe they are getting high off the plastic?

One of them has a large chunk of twisted ropes in its mouth and is tugging away at it, trying to free it from the pile. It pulls and pulls until it eventually tears it free. And it is then that I see it, a thin gnarly branch of a tree poking up through the nets... my log was here, right next to me, all along! I let out a hearty laugh as I reflect on my moments of panic, that my log had deserted me, or worse, that I was imagining the whole thing. My laugh quickly turns to an insane giggle as I frantically search for something to cut the nets with, something to cut her free with. I walk no more than five paces when I see a broken beer bottle half buried in the sand. I dig it out gingerly and pick it up by the neck and stand up, holding the bottle out.

Just then I see an old Thai man standing on the sand bank looking at me. He is bent over from age or from bracing himself against a gale force wind that was no longer there. He is leaning on a stick he must have picked up. His eyes are smiling but his face is drawn tight, the many wrinkles, cracks and creases somehow locking it into place.

I look up at him, a crazy grin on my face, caked in sand, my hair standing up and out at all angles, my fisherman's pants hanging down limp and wet from the battering, my t-shirt long since gone. I feel not just lightheaded, but simply light. I feel like dancing, and as we stand there regarding each other I wonder what it is he sees. Then I notice he has a few wild beach dogs around him, which seemed to have followed him there, their noses to the ground, their ears pricked, their mangy fur bristling with the gusts of wind. The main dog, the top dog, was a white, patchy Thai native dog with most of its fur missing, lots of scars and a withering stare that said 'you fuck with me and you'll know it'. It stood next to the man and they both stared at me. Nothing in it, just curiosity at what the crazy looking *Farang* was doing. Next thing I know my legs are moving and my hips are swinging and I am dancing, smiling at the old man and the dog. I dance over to the log, a broken bottle in my hand, with a grin that could light Patong on a Friday night. I stop when I get there, wink at the old man and the dog, and commence slashing away at the nets that had trapped my log in a suffocating series of knots and twists that would only tighten with time – the kind of knots that set like rock and cannot be undone. I laugh crazily as I tear sections of the net off my precious log. The birds had left when I started and now they return, somehow sensing my harmlessness amidst the slashing fury. Maybe they thought they had found a brother, another one dazzled by shiny things...

I slow down my pace as I near the surface of one of the branches and gently shoo one of the gulls off the protruding branch as I cut the last layer off, freeing it at last. I look at it lovingly and run my hand along its surface. The bottle falls from my other hand and I look up at the old man again, as if to say, 'Look at this! What a little gem, hey?'

The old man just looks at me and I can see the beginnings of a smile insinuate itself on his cracked, withered face and then it is there, transforming the hard features into those of a small child's, his eyes shine out from their sockets like torches at night and I know right then that it is going to be OK, it is all going to be OK. I am alright, a bit nuts, weary and broken, but OK. I thank him silently for something he probably has no idea he has done and turn my attention back to the log as he and his dogs shuffle away up the beach.

The tangle of nets and ropes seems to go on forever. I carefully cut down the main trunk, hoping that I can just peel it all off and reveal the sleeping beauty beneath it... The tangle is almost impenetrable and I put more weight behind the slashing until I can feel the warm blood running from the hand grasping the broken bottle. I hadn't noticed the neck was broken as well and it had been ripping into me all this time. *How many times had I discovered my right arm bleeding over the years since the accident?* The burns were the worst, often it would be the sound of burning flesh that I heard before the feeling that should've been there but wasn't, it being scraped away years ago by surgeons. A thousand years ago, it seemed now.

As I cut away, the trunk reveals itself. A series of rolling twists so beautiful and fluid they take my breath away. I grin at them with such joy that it feels like I am going to burst. Then I go to work on the other main branch. I can see the thick base of it coming out of the trunk directly opposite the other one, about two thirds of the way up the trunk. I can see it, through the jumble of nylon nets hanging off it like a drunk girl's evening dress at the end of the night.

I am struck again by the thought of my father smashing his way into my 4-year-old psyche without a care or a thought in the world, blundering haphazardly through my early memories. Sometimes he was just a shadow on the edge of things. It was maybe two years after he left that I stopped looking for him at the football club trophy nights. Like all the other boys, looking for a Dad that just wasn't there. It was probably 5 years later that I stopped brawling at school as a result of the taunts of being a 'girl', that I was going turn gay, as if this was all it took. And every punch that landed on me was like fuel for the fire that would burn fiercely enough to eventually make my opponents think twice about it. Being small in stature I had developed a cold, fierce and, at the same time, dead stare that was relentless in intensity and focus. The same way I looked at the balls my brother and I threw at each other in playful sporting combat.

When it comes to it, it is easier than I thought. I kneel on the pile of fishing nets and I forgive him. I forgive his idiocy, his mindlessness, his selfishness. I forgive his actions and his lack of action. And after all this crying, I don't shed even one tear. I pause momentarily and stare out at the *dton sun* trees that enclose the beach and listen to my forgiveness being swept away with the wind, a broken bottle in my hand and a stunned reaction to the simplicity of it all.

I resume my slashing and tearing of the nets until I am down to a few centimetres of cover. I turn the bottle around in my hand and place it at the top of the log and gently run it down through the twisted remainder of nets, through my legs and down the entire length of it. The net springs back, and there she is.

The twisted trunk looks like the chords of a great song, some flow about the coercion of each part becoming one thing of absolute tortured beauty. The branches spring out like open arms waiting for a hug, their thick bases ending in an almost impossible delicacy, like the hands of a fat pianist. I run my hands along each one simultaneously, amazed at how a thing of such fragility could have remained intact after years of being bounced and thrown around in monsoonal waters.

But she had made it. We both had made it.

I drop the bottle and listen as it comes to rest in the pile of discarded nets. It is the clearest sound I had ever heard in my life and it seems to dance with the hiss and rumble of the waves. It too disappears into the trees.

I let my arms continue travelling down and around the huge trunk and as I hug her I realise how similar it is to the tree root I had found with Phee Noi all those years ago. As I lie down it is as if the branches curl around my body, holding me against the trunk until I dissolve into it. Grinning to myself I close my eyes.

I am a lucky man.